SAINT PETER'S SNOW

SAINT PETER'S SNOW

Leo Perutz

Translated from the German
by Eric Mosbacher

Arcade Publishing • New York

First North American Edition 1990

Published in Austria by Paul Zsolnay Verlag, Vienna under the title
Sankt Petri-Schnee

Arcade Publishing books may be purchased in bulk at special discounts
for sales promotion, corporate gifts, fund-raising, or educational purposes.
Special editions can also be created to specifications. For details, contact the
Special Sales Department, Arcade Publishing, 307 West 36th Street, 11th
Floor, New York, NY 10018 or arcade@skyhorsepublishing.com.

Arcade Publishing® is a registered trademark of Skyhorse Publishing,
Inc.®, a Delaware corporation.

Visit our website at www.arcadepub.com.

10 9 8 7 6 5 4 3 2 1

Library of Congress Cataloging-in-Publication Data is available on file.

Cover design by Robert Reed
Cover illustration by Tamara de Lempicka: *Le Docteur Boucard*, 1928. From
a private collection. © by DACS, 1990

ISBN: 978-1-61145-886-2
Ebook ISBN: 978-1-62872-507-0

Printed in the United States of America

*Dedicated to the memory
of one who reached perfection
and departed early*

ONE

When the night released me I was a nameless, impersonal something with no conception of past or future. I lay, perhaps for many hours, perhaps only for a fraction of a second, in a state that was a kind of insensibility, which then gave way to something I can no longer describe. If I call it a shadowy awareness of myself coupled with a sense of being totally undefined, I have inadequately indicated its special and peculiar quality. It would be easy to say that I floated in a void, but those words mean nothing. All I knew was that something existed, but I did not know that it was myself.

I have no idea how long that lasted, or when the first memories came back. They popped up inside me and promptly faded again, I could not hold them. One of them, in spite of its nebulous nature, was painful or frightening – I heard myself breathing heavily, as if I were having a nightmare.

The first memories that stuck were completely trivial. The name of a dog I had owned for a short time occurred to me. Then I remembered that someone to whom I had lent a volume of my edition of Shakespeare had never returned it. Then the name of a street and the number of a house in it flashed through my mind, though I could not connect it with anything in my life, and then I saw a motorcyclist with two dead hares on his back driving along the deserted village street – when had that been? I remembered stumbling and falling as I avoided him, and when I got up I noticed that I was holding my watch, it was just eight o'clock, and in falling I had broken the glass. I had dashed out of the house without hat or coat and with the watch in my hand . . .

That was the point I had reached when the events of the previous weeks came crashing down on me with indescribable violence, the beginning, the end and everything in between at the same time. They came crashing down on me like the beams and masonry of a collapsing house. I saw the people and the things I had lived among, they were immeasurably huge and eerie, gigantic and terrifying, like people and things from another world. And there was something inside me that was about to explode with devastating effect; the idea of a happiness, or some fear connected with it, or despair and agonising desire – all those words are weak and feeble. It was the thought of something that could not be borne even for a second.

That was the first encounter of my awakened consciousness with the tremendous experience that lay behind me.

It was too much for me. I heard myself shriek, and I must have tried to throw off the blanket, for I felt a stabbing pain in my upper arm, and I succumbed to – no, I took refuge in – a faint that was my salvation.

When I awoke for the second time it was broad daylight. This time self-awareness arrived without any transition. I realised I was in a hospital room, a friendly, well furnished room obviously intended for paying or otherwise privileged patients. An elderly nurse sitting by the window was crocheting and occasionally sipped a cup of coffee. In a bed against the opposite wall was a man with a stubbly chin and sunken cheeks, and his head was covered in white bandages. His big, sad eyes were fixed on me, and there was a worried look on his face. I think that for a few moments I may have caught sight of myself in a mirror as I lay there, pale, emaciated, unshaven and with my head bandaged, but it may have been a patient who shared my room while I was unconscious. In that case he must have been moved from the room in the next few minutes without my noticing it, because when I opened my eyes again he and his bed had gone.

Now I could remember everything. The events that had brought me here stood out in my mind sharply and clearly, and now I saw them in a different light. Their oppressive, monstrous quality had gone. Much of what I had been through still struck me as weird, much of it was puzzling and inexplicable. But nothing that had happened frightened me, and the people involved no longer loomed in my mind as huge, terrifying phantoms. In the bright light of day they were of human proportions, they were human beings like me and everyone else, they were creatures of this world. Almost unnoticeably and as a matter of course they linked up with my previous existence, the days, the people and the things, they merged with them, were part of my life and were inseparable from it.

The nurse noticed that I was awake and rose to her feet. Her expression was one of smug simplicity, and as I watched her now I was struck by her resemblance to the old woman who had suddenly emerged like a fury from the crowd of angry, protesting peasants and threatened the old priest with a bread-knife. "Death to the priest," she had yelled, and it seemed strange that she should now be in my room, simply, quietly and demurely looking after me. But when she came closer the resemblance vanished. I had made a mistake. When she reached my bedside I saw that her face was that of a total stranger. I had never seen the woman before.

She noticed that I wanted to say something and raised her hands in a gesture indicating that I should spare myself the effort, as talking was not good for me. At that moment I had a sensation of *déjà vu*, the feeling that all this – the bed, the hospital room, the nurse – was not new to me and that I had been through it all before. That, too, was an illusion, of course, but the reality behind it was no less strange. I now remembered that in the Westphalian village where I was the doctor I had frequently had a kind of second sight, foreseeing in many respects the circumstances in which I now found myself. That was the truth, I could swear to it. Such phenomena have been noted in Westphalia since time out of mind.

"How did I get here?" I asked.

She shrugged her shoulders. Perhaps that was a matter she had been forbidden to talk to me about.

"How long have I been here?" I persisted.

She seemed to be thinking it over.

"This is the fifth week," she replied after a while.

That was impossible, I realised. Outside it was snowing, it was still winter. I must have been brought here only a few days ago – four or perhaps five. It had been snowing that Sunday, my last day in Morwede, and it was still snowing. Why was she lying to me?

"That can't be right," I said. "You're not telling me the truth."

She looked perplexed.

"It may be six weeks," she said hesitantly. "I'm not sure. This is my fifth week in this room. Before that another nurse was here. You were here when I came."

"What's the date today?" I asked.

She acted as if she had not understood.

"What's the date today? What's today's date?" I repeated.

"March 2nd 1932," she said eventually.

March 2nd. This time she was telling the truth, I could tell. The date fitted in with my calculations. I had started work as the village doctor at Morwede on January 25th, and had worked for a month in that small Westphalian village before that ill-fated Sunday. I had been here for five days, now I was sure of it. Why had she lied to me, and who had told her to? In whose interest was it to make me believe I had lain unconscious in this hospital bed for five whole weeks? There was no point in pressing the woman any further. When she realised I was not going to ask her any more questions, she told me of her own accord that I had regained consciousness several times. Once, when she had dropped a bowl while changing my bandages, I had asked who was there, without opening my eyes. Later I

4

had several times complained of pain, and also asked for something to drink, but each time had promptly relapsed into a coma. I could not remember any of this.

"Very few do remember afterwards," she said, and went back to her seat by the window and her crochet work.

I lay with my eyes closed, thinking about what had now come to an end – come to an end for ever. She was alive, I knew, she had escaped the dreadful last hours and the retribution – my certainty of this was as solid as a rock. The bullet meant for her had struck me. People of her kind did not perish. Whatever she did, no matter how great the guilt she took upon herself, there would always be someone to fling himself between her and avenging fate.

But I also knew that it was over, and that she would not return. Her path would not lead her to me a second time. Never mind. She had been mine for one night, and that night remained with me, no one could take it away from me, it was embedded in my life like dark red almandine in a piece of granite. That night had linked me with her for ever. I had held her in my arms, felt her breath and her heart-beat and the trembling of her limbs, seen the childish laughter with which she woke. No, it was not over. What a woman gives in such a tremendous night she gives for ever. Perhaps she was someone else's now – I could contemplate the possibility without sorrow. Farewell, Bibiche.

Bibiche was the name she used when she talked to herself. "Poor Bibiche." How often had I heard those affectionately complaining words on her lips. "You're angry with me and I don't know why. Poor Bibiche." That was what she wrote in a note that a small boy brought me – how long ago had that been? And once, when we hardly knew each other, at the time when she acted as if she were indifferent to me and had accidentally burnt her hand with a drop of acid, she had looked at her little finger in pained surprise and exclaimed: "It hurts, you're unkind to Bibiche." I laughed at her, and she looked at me coldly and dismissively. But that was all over, and I should never see that look again. It had been all over since that night . . .

I heard footsteps and opened my eyes. The medical superintendent and his two assistants were standing by my bed, and behind them a man of Herculean proportions in a blue and white striped coat was pushing the bandage trolley through the door.

In spite of his disguise I recognised him at once. The huge, powerful body, the weak, receding chin, the deep-set, watery blue eyes were those of Prince Praxatin, the last of the house of Rurik. He had grown a moustache, so I could not see the scar on his upper lip, his flaxen hair fell over his brow instead of being brushed straight back, and his hands were brown and uncared for – was it he or wasn't it? It was he, there was no doubt about it. The way he tried to avoid my eyes told me everything. He had found a safe refuge here, playing the part of a hospital porter under an assumed name, and did not want to be recognised. Well, so far as I was concerned he could continue his pitiful existence as long as his conscience allowed him to, I had no intention of giving him away, he had nothing to fear from me.

I heard the medical superintendent's voice.

"Awake? Good morning," he said. "How do you feel? Better? Any pain?"

I did not answer, but went on staring at Prince Praxatin. This made him feel uncomfortable, and he had turned away; now I saw something I had not seen before, a bright red scar that began behind his right ear and extended to near his chin – a reminder of the night on which he betrayed his friend and benefactor.

"Do you know where you are?" the medical superintendent asked.

I looked him in the face. He was a man of about fifty, with lively eyes and a beard flecked with grey. He obviously wanted to find out whether my mind was clear yet.

"In a hospital," I said.

6

"Quite right," he said. "You're in the town hospital at Osnabrück."

One of the two assistants bent over me.

"Do you recognise me, Amberg?" he asked.

"No," I said. "Who are you?"

"But you must remember me," he went on. "Think again. We both worked for six months in the Bacteriological Institute in Berlin. Have I really changed so much that you don't recognise me?"

"Are you Dr Friebe?" I asked tentatively.

"So you do recognise me. At last," he said with satisfaction, and began removing the bandage from my upper arm and shoulder.

This Dr Friebe had been a colleague of mine at the Bacteriological Institute, and he knew her too. I badly wanted to hear her name on his lips, but some instinct told me not to mention her.

I pointed to the bullet wound on my arm.

"Was it a bullet wound?" I asked.

"What did you say?" he said with his mind on what he was doing.

"Did you have to extract the bullet?"

He looked at me in surprise.

"What bullet are you talking about?" he said. "You have lacerations and contusions on your arm and shoulder."

I grew angry.

"Lacerations and contusions?" I exclaimed. "That's nonsense. The arm wound is the result of a revolver shot and the shoulder wound is the result of a stab. Even a layman could see that. And besides . . ."

The medical superintendent now intervened.

"What are you suggesting?" he said. "When pedestrians ignore their instructions our traffic police don't attack them with knives and revolvers."

"What do you mean?" I interrupted.

"You must remember that just five weeks ago at two o'clock

in the afternoon you were standing as if in a trance in the middle of heavy traffic in the station square here in Osnabrück and you didn't move though the policeman directing the traffic and the drivers yelled at you, but you took no notice . . ."

"That's right," I said. "I saw a green Cadillac."

"Good gracious," the medical superintendent exclaimed. "It's true that there's only that one Cadillac here in Osnabrück, but for you, coming from Berlin, a Cadillac's no novelty. You must have seen any number of Cadillacs."

"Yes, but that one . . ."

"And what happened then?" he interrupted me.

"I crossed the square towards the station, bought a ticket and got into the train."

"No," said the medical superintendent. "You never reached the station. You walked straight into a car and were knocked down. The base of the skull was broken and there was brain haemorrhage, and that was the state you were in when you were brought here. You were in a bad way, the outcome might have been different, but now you're out of danger."

I tried to read his face. He could not have seriously meant what he said, it was absurd. I had got into the train, read two newspapers and a magazine, and dropped off to sleep. I woke up when the train stopped at Münster and got out and bought cigarettes on the platform. I arrived at Rheda at about five o'clock, when it was beginning to get dark, and from there I went on in a sleigh.

"I beg your pardon," I said quite diffidently, "but the head wound is the result of a blow with a blunt instrument. It was done with a flail."

"What are you saying?" he exclaimed. "Where on earth is threshing still done with a flail? Machinery is used everywhere in the country nowadays."

What was I to answer? He was not to know that there was no machinery on Baron von Malchin's estate, where the corn was still sown, cut and threshed as it was a hundred years ago.

"Where I was until five days ago they still use flails," I said eventually.

He exchanged glances with Dr Friebe.

"Where you were until five days ago?" he said incredulously. "Really? Well, it will have been as you said. A blow with a flail. Very well, don't worry about it. Such unpleasant experiences with flails are best forgotten. Try to switch off, you need rest. You must tell me all about it another time."

He turned to the nurse.

"Biscuits, tea with milk, sieved vegetables," he told her, and he left, followed by his two assistants. The last to leave was Prince Praxatin, pushing the bandage trolley. He cast me a timid glance.

What was the meaning of this? Was the medical superintendent play-acting for my benefit, or did he really believe in that car accident? What had happened had been quite different, as he very well knew.

TWO

My name is Georg Friedrich Amberg and I am a physician. That is how the report on the events at Morwede that I shall write one day when I am physically fit enough will begin. But that will not be just yet. I am not in a state to put pen to paper – I've been told to rest and to switch off, and in any case I can't use my injured arm. All I can do is to imprint in my memory every single thing that happened and hold it fast, so as not to lose even the most insignificant detail. For the time being that is all I can do.

I shall have to go a long way back in my story. My mother died a few months after I was born. My father was a historian of repute. His speciality was the history of Germany up to the Great Interregnum. In his last years he lectured at a university in central Germany on the investiture struggle, on German military organisation at the end of the thirteenth century, on the meaning and significance of feudal tenure, and on the administrative reforms of Frederick II. When he died I was fourteen. He left nothing but a handsome but rather limited library – apart from the classics, it consisted of historical works only. I still have some of his books.

I was looked after by a maternal aunt. She was a pedantically strict, reticent woman who rarely came out of her shell, and we had little to say to each other. But I shall be grateful to her all my life. I hardly ever heard a friendly word from her, but she managed her slender means so well that she enabled me to complete my education. Even as a boy I was fascinated by my father's subject, history, and there was hardly a book in his library that I had not read several times. But shortly before my school-leaving exam, when I announced that I wanted to be a historian, i.e., an academic, my aunt vigorously opposed it. To her pragmatic mind historical research was a vague and useless activity, remote from the problems of real life. She insisted on my going in for a practical profession, with my feet firmly planted on the ground, as she put it. That meant either medicine or the law.

I jibbed at this, and the result was violent arguments. One day my aunt in her pedantic way worked out with pencil and paper the financial sacrifices she had made for my sake in the course of years. At that I gave in – what else could I do? She certainly had my welfare at heart and had undergone real deprivations for my sake, and I could not disappoint her. So I became a medical student.

Six years later I was a doctor of average knowledge and ability, like hundreds of others. I had had a year's hospital experience, and had no patients, no money and no connections and, worst of all, no sense of vocation for medicine.

As the result of an experience to which I shall return later, during my last year as a medical student I had adopted certain habits that I could not really afford. Wherever the fashionable world went, I went too. Extravagant I was not, but this change of life-style involved extra expense which the occasional fee I earned from private tutoring was insufficient to cover. So I often had to sell valuable books from my father's library. In early January that year I was once more financially embarrassed. I had a number of small debts I could not meet. Shakespeare and Molière were the only classics left in my father's library, and I took them to a second-hand bookseller who was a friend of mine.

He offered me what I thought was a fair price, but he called me back from the doorway and pointed out that the Shakespeare was incomplete – the volume containing the Sonnets and *The Winter's Tale* was missing. For a moment I was dismayed, because I knew it was not at home, but then I remembered that I had lent it to a colleague some months before. I asked the bookseller to wait till the afternoon and went off to get it back.

My colleague was out, so I decided to wait for him. Out of sheer boredom I picked up the morning newspaper that was lying on the table.

It is not without a certain interest to put yourself back into the situation you were in during the minutes immediately before an unexpected event that turned out to be a crucial point in your life – to ask yourself where you were and what you were thinking about. Well, I was sitting in an unheated room, freezing in my light-weight overcoat, for I could not afford a proper winter coat. Without particular interest and just to pass the time, I read a story about the arrest of a man accused of attempted murder in a train, an article on the nutritional value of coffee, and another on apparatus gymnastics. I was annoyed with my colleague for his irresponsible failure to return the book, and also by a grease mark on the page of the newspaper I was reading – obviously my colleague had been reading it at breakfast and bread-and-butter had come into contact with it.

The next thing that happened was banal, almost to the point of triviality. My eyes fell on an advertisement, that was all.

The administration of Baron von Malchin's estate at Morwede, district of Rheda, Westphalia, invited applications for the position of village doctor, minimum income guaranteed, together with free accommodation and heating, preference given to applicants with a good all-round education.

It did not strike me immediately that I might be a possible candidate for the job. What attracted my attention was the estate owner's name. I found myself muttering Baron von Malchin and von der Bork, and it struck me that it was the word Malchin that had reminded me of the full name and title, that it was familiar to me, though I could not remember where I had heard or read it.

I pondered. My memory sometimes follows strange paths. A tune occurred to me, an old song I had not thought of for many years. I hummed it, and then hummed it again, and I was back in the oak-panelled room with the table loaded with books, and I was sitting at the piano and playing the song, and then the words, which were banal enough, came back to me: "Your love is all I need, I do not ask for more," they began. My father was pacing up and down the room, with his hands clasped behind his back, as usual, and a chaffinch was twittering in the garden. I went on playing. "It's not for me to plead for faithfulness as well," the song went on. "Baron von Malchin and von der Bork," a voice announced. My father stopped and said: "Ask him in," and I got up and left the room, as I always did when my father had a visitor.

It only occurred to me much later that that visitor and the owner of the estate at Morwede were not necessarily the same person, there might be a number of persons with that name. I read the advertisement again. Then I went to the desk and wrote a letter applying for the job, briefly mentioning my father; I left a brief note asking my colleague to return the book immediately, and went to the nearest post office and posted the letter.

There was no answer for ten days, but when at last it came it was satisfactory enough. Baron von Malchin wrote that he regarded it as an honour to have known my father personally, and he was happy to be able to be of service to the son of a scholar whom he highly esteemed and whose premature death he deplored. He wanted to know whether I would be able to start work that month. I would have to travel via Osnabrück and Münster, and a car would be waiting for me at Rheda station. There were some formalities to be observed. Would I please send my medical diploma and confirmation of my year's hospital experience to the office of the local authority.

When I told my aunt that I would be leaving Berlin that same month and beginning work in the country, she accepted it as a matter of course and as something she had been looking forward to for a long time. All we talked about that evening was the immediate practical things that had to be done, such as completing my wardrobe and procuring the necessary surgical and obstetric instruments and a supply of medicines. There was still some jewellery left by my mother: an emerald ring, two bracelets and a couple of old-fashioned earrings. We turned all this into cash, but the amount failed to come up to expectations and so, painful as I found it, I had to sell many more of my father's books.

On January 25th my aunt came with me to the station, and she insisted on paying for the provisions for my journey. When I said goodbye to her on the platform and thanked her for everything I saw something like emotion on her face for the first time, and I think she even had tears in her eyes. When I got into the train she turned resolutely and walked away without looking back. That was what she was like.

At midday I arrived at Osnabrück.

THREE

I used the hour and a half wait for my connection to walk round the town. There is an old square there called the Great Freedom of the Cathedral and a sixteenth-century fortified tower called Civil Obedience. My curiosity was aroused by these two apparently conflicting names between which there nevertheless seemed to me to be some connection, and I made my way towards the Old Town. But chance willed it that I saw neither the square nor the tower.

Was it really chance? I have heard that it is possible to set ships in motion and steer them from a distance of many kilometres by means of electric waves. What unknown force was it that took control of me and caused me to forget what I was looking for and to make my way through the winding streets of the Old Town as if I had a definite objective, and to go through the doorway – it was the doorway of a house through which there was a public right of way – leading to a little square with a stone saint in the middle and pork butchers' and greengrocers' stalls all round it? I crossed the square, went up some steps, turned into a narrow side street, and stopped outside an old curiosity shop. I thought I was looking at a shop window, and did not know I was looking into the future. But why an unknown will granted me this peep into the future I do not know and cannot explain to the present day.

It was chance, of course, nothing but chance. I have no inclination to ascribe ordinary events to transcendental causes, I refuse on principle thus to attribute to things an importance to which they are not entitled. I prefer sticking to solid facts.

There are certainly many old curiosity shops in the Old Town and I had stopped in front of one of them, the first to which I came. Among all the bric-à-brac in the window, the glasses, the Roman copper coins, the wood-carvings, the porcelain figures, there was nothing surprising in the fact that a marble relief attracted my attention, it was bound to do so because of its size alone. It was obviously a copy of a mediaeval work and represented a man's head – a head with bold, almost wild and yet noble features. On his lips there was the fixed, remote smile to be seen on all Gothic carvings, but I knew that this was not the first time I had set eyes on that disproportionately long face furrowed by passion and its strong but finely formed brow. I had seen it before somewhere, I had come across it in a book, perhaps, or on a cameo, but whose face it was I could not remember, and the longer I looked at it the more uneasy I felt. I knew that those powerful features would not let me go, but would follow me into my dreams. Suddenly this carving filled me with a childish fear. I didn't want to look at it any longer, and turned away.

My eyes fell on a pile of dusty books and papers held together by a piece of string. I could see the title of the top book, which was *Why is Belief in God Disappearing from the World?*

What a strange question. Was it justified, stated like that? And at what poor and inadequate answers had the writer arrived? What commonplaces did he offer the reader? Did he blame science? Technology? Socialism? Or ultimately even the Church itself?

Though all this was basically a matter of indifference to me, I could not dismiss the book from my mind or the question its title asked. I was in an unusually nervy state. Perhaps it was anxiety about the new environment in which I was about to be plunged, perhaps I was nervous about life in the country and a job I did not feel up to – perhaps it was this suppressed fear that made me seek a diversion for my thoughts. I felt I must find out now, straight away, why belief in God was disappearing from the world. It was obsessive. I wanted to go into the shop and buy the book – I was prepared to buy the whole pile of books and pamphlets if the dealer refused to sell me that single item – but it did not come to that, because the shop was shut.

It was the midday break. I had not thought of that. The dealer had gone home for lunch. I felt hungry myself, and my mood went from bad to worse. Was I to wait until he chose to come back and open up again – and perhaps end by missing my train? Why had I walked into the town instead of remaining at the station and quietly eating my lunch? That would have spared me all this annoyance. The shop owner might come back at any moment, of course, no doubt he lived somewhere in the neighbourhood, in one of those tall, airless houses with dirty grey façades and windows covered with grime, he was probably sitting behind one of them hurriedly eating his lunch – or perhaps he had not left the building at all but had gone into another room and locked the door to avoid being disturbed during his meal.

I noticed a bell-pull by the door and pulled it, but no one answered.

So he's having his midday snooze, I said to myself angrily, and suddenly I had a clear picture of him in my mind. He was a bald old man with a stubbly beard, and was lying on a sofa, snoring. He had drawn the blanket up to his chin, his greasy stiff hat was hanging on a nail by the door, and he was fast asleep, leaving me to wait until he came round. I shall do nothing of the sort, I said to myself. Why isn't he in his shop just at the time when strangers are around? He doesn't seem to care very much about disposing of his wares. Very well, then. I don't have to buy the book.

I took one more nervous, surreptitious look at the Gothic relief, as if I were doing something guilty, and left.

When I got as far as the passage through the house it occurred to me that I could have the book sent to me. There was not much time to spare, but I hurried back. The shop was still shut, but I noted the name and address.

The man's name was Gerson, and very likely the book is still in his window. I could have spared myself the trouble of going back, because I never ordered it. I could not foresee that I would find the answer at Morwede to the two questions that plagued me, why belief in God was disappearing from the world and who the dead man was whose features were reproduced on the marble relief.

Ten minutes before the train left I was in the station square, and it was there that I had that unexpected encounter with the green Cadillac. To put it in a nutshell, it came from the right while I was waiting for a signal from the policeman directing the traffic. A woman was at the wheel, a woman I knew.

FOUR

Now, lying in this hospital bed with my right arm stretched out on the bed-cover as if I were asleep or anaesthetised and my eyes seeking for a resting place among the red lines and angles and stars of the pattern on the wall – now, at this insignificant moment, I feel my heart beating and my breath stopping just because I'm thinking of Bibiche. But then, in the station square, I was quite calm – in fact I was surprised at how calmly I took it. I think I felt the encounter to be not remarkable in the least but perfectly natural, and the only surprise was that it had taken place so late, at the last moment, in fact.

In Berlin I had been looking vainly for a whole year for this woman at the wheel of a green Cadillac. And now, just when I was about to begin a new life of which I had few expectations and hardly any hopes – the future seemed to offer me nothing but a grey and pleasureless monotony – the city that I was leaving as one leaves a cold and selfish lover, the city with its hard and hostile features for the first time showed me a kind and gentle smile. See what I have for you, it called after me. You see that I think of you. And you want to leave me? Was I to turn and go back? In that case it was too late. Was that the meaning of this encounter? Or was it only a parting message from the world I was leaving behind, a mocking farewell, a last fleeting wave from the other bank?

It was neither the one nor the other. It was a finding again and a prelude to something bigger. But that was something I dared not think about.

★

At first all that was known about her at the Bacteriological Institute was that her name was Kallisto Tsanaris and that her subject was biochemistry, and what we found out about her later was little enough. She had been brought to Berlin from Athens at the age of twelve and lived with her mother, who seemed to be an invalid, in a villa in the Zoo quarter. She moved only in the most exalted circles. Her father, a colonel in the Greek army who had been aide-de-camp to the king, was dead.

That was the extent of our information, and we had to be content with it, for she talked to none of us about her personal affairs. She kept a certain distance between herself and everyone else and, if she ever exchanged a few words with anyone, it would be exclusively about practical matters, such as a bunsen burner that was not working properly or the desirability of procuring another high pressure steriliser.

On her first appearance in the institute everyone sat up and took notice, and we all did our best to make an impression on her. She was paid every possible kind of attention, she was asked about her scientific interests and plans, and she was offered advice and help. Later, when we realised that all these approaches were met with the same cool indifference and reserve, interest in her diminished, though it did not completely disappear. She was said to be proud and arrogant, spoilt and calculating and, of course, stupid. In her eyes academics did not count, it was said – to be noticed by her you had to own at least a Mercedes. In fact her disinclination to any form of friendly contact seemed to be restricted to the laboratory. When she left in the evening there would always be a cavalier waiting to help her into his car. Each of these admirers had his own car, and we got to know them all by sight and had appropriate nicknames for them. It would be known, for instance, that on the previous evening she had been called for by the Patriarch Abraham, or had been seen in a box at the opera with the Grinning Faun. The Patriarch Abraham was a white-bearded old gentleman of distinctly Semitic appearance, and the

Grinning Faun a very young man with a perpetual smile who always seemed to be enjoying himself. There were also the so-called Mexican Brewer, the Big Game Hunter and the Kalmuck Prince. One evening when she had been working late the Big Game Hunter appeared in the laboratory and asked for her. We knew she was in the changing room, but we treated the man as an unwelcome intruder and told him severely that persons unconnected with the institute were not allowed in the laboratory, and that he must wait outside. He took this quietly and left – greatly to my disappointment, for I had the reputation of being a first class fencer and would have dearly loved to cross swords with him, not so much out of jealousy as because I hoped in this way to play a part in her thoughts or at least draw attention to me.

Towards the end of the term I was ill for a few days and had to stay at home, and when I returned to work she had left. She had finished the work she was engaged on, and I was told that she had said goodbye to every single one of her colleagues and had even asked after me. She had mentioned her future plans only in the vaguest way, and the general view in the institute was that she had given up her studies and was about to get married to the so-called Kalmuck Prince. I did not believe this, because she had seemed exceptionally keen on her research work and betrayed a quite unusual, almost morbid ambition. Moreover, the individual whom we called the Kalmuck Prince had not been seen waiting for her outside the institute for two months. He and his smart Hispano seemed to have fallen out of favour.

For six months I had worked in the same room with her from morning till late afternoon, and for the whole of that time, unless my memory deceives me, I had not exchanged more than ten words with her, apart from good morning and good night.

At first I was convinced she would turn up in the laboratory with a new research project. I was unable to believe that the time when I had been able to see her every day, hear her voice, follow her walk and her movements with my eyes, was over for good. Only after weeks of vain waiting did I begin to look for her.

No doubt there are exact and reliable ways of tracing a person in Berlin, discovering his or her address and daily habits. A private detective agency would probably have taken only a day or two to do this. I had to set about it differently. My meeting with her had to be by pure chance, or at any rate that is what it had to seem to be.

In the evening I walked through smart restaurants even the names of which I had never heard of before. When you have no intention of remaining in a place like that, you have the feeling that you are attracting attention and mistrust even before you walk in. I generally acted as if I were looking for a free table or a friend whom I was expecting. When waiters approached I would mention a made-up name such as Herr Konsul Stockström or Herr Assessor Bauschlot and would be told they were sorry, they didn't know the gentleman, and I would walk out looking peeved. Sometimes I would order some little thing. On one such occasion the waiter surprised me with the information that Herr Konsul Stockström had just left – "a tall, thin gentleman, isn't he, sir, with horn-rimmed spectacles and hair parted in the middle".

I looked for Bibiche among the couples at *thés dansants* in the big hotels, I waited to see the cars drive up at theatres on first nights, I went to the private view when art exhibitions were opened, and I was among the invited guests when new films were shown. With a great deal of trouble I managed to secure an invitation to a reception at the Greek embassy, and when she was not there I felt disheartened for the first time.

I remembered that a colleague had told me he had once seen her in a bar. I went there and became a regular customer. I sat there for hours over a cocktail, night after night, with my eyes fixed on the door, waiting for her to walk in. At first, whenever it opened I felt a slight shudder of expectation, but later I did not even look up. Without noticing it, I had grown accustomed to the sight of people of no interest to me coming through it.

The results of my searches were more than paltry. I had a number of popular dance tunes in my head and I knew the names of most of the new plays. But I had not seen Bibiche.

Once I saw the Big Game Hunter. He was sitting alone at a table in a wine bar, smoking a big cigar and gazing straight ahead of him. He looked noticeably older. Seeing him sitting alone like that, I had the quite definite feeling that he too had lost track of Bibiche and was chasing after her in his roadster all over Berlin, always on the look-out and always restless. I suddenly felt sympathy for the man I had once wanted to cross swords with and nearly rose and shook hands with him. We were fellow-sufferers after all. He did not recognise me, but my searching gaze seemed to make him feel uncomfortable. He changed his seat and sat so that I could not see his face. Then he took a newspaper from his pocket and began to read.

I looked for Bibiche until the very last day. Strangely, the idea that she might have left Berlin did not occur to me until I got to the station and asked for a ticket to Osnabrück.

And at Osnabrück I saw her in the station square. The green Cadillac she was driving stopped barely ten paces away from me. She wore a sealskin coat and a grey Basque beret.

At that moment I was happy, completely happy. I did not even want to be seen and recognised by her, it was enough that she was there and that I saw her. The whole thing lasted only a few seconds, I think. She adjusted her beret, threw away a cigarette stub and drove off.

Only when she moved slowly away and then accelerated did I realise I ought to do something, jump in a taxi and follow her, no, not to speak to her but only to avoid losing sight of her again. I wanted to know where she was going and where she lived. At the same time I realised that I was no longer a master of my time, that I had undertaken an obligation. My train was leaving in a few minutes and a car would be waiting for me at Rheda station. Never mind, you must follow her, a voice inside me cried. But it was too late. The green car disappeared into one of the wide streets leading to the town centre.

Farewell, Bibiche, I muttered to myself. This is the second time I've lost you. Fate gave me a chance, and I missed it. Fate? Why fate? God put you in my way, Bibiche, God, not fate. The question why belief in God was disappearing from the world shot through my mind, and for a moment I saw in my mind's eye the staring marble face in the antique dealer's window.

I started, and looked about me. I was standing in the middle of the square and there was a terrible din all round me, taxi drivers shouted at me, a motorcyclist dismounted right in front of me, swore and shook his fist at me, the policeman regulating the traffic signalled to me several times, but I could not make out what he wanted me to do – was I to stop or go on, or go right or left?

I stepped to the right, and dropped the newspapers and magazine I had under my arm. I bent to pick them up, but there was a honk behind me and I jumped aside. No, I must have picked them up, because later I read them in the train. I picked them up and jumped aside, and then – what happened?

Nothing at all. I reached the pavement, took my ticket, and collected my luggage, all that's obvious. And then I got into the train.

FIVE

At Rheda station a big four-seater sleigh was waiting for me.
A lad who did not look in the least like a coachman to the
nobility took charge of my luggage. I turned up my coat collar
and pulled the rug over my knees, and off we went through
flat, desolate country between bare roadside trees and across
snow-covered fields of stubble. The dreary monotony of the
landscape was oppressive, and the failing light increased my
gloom. Travelling always makes me drowsy, and I fell asleep.
When the sleigh drew up at the forester's lodge I woke up. I
heard a dog barking, and when I sleepily opened my eyes the
man who now sweeps the floor in my hospital room and
behaves as if he had never seen me before was standing by the
sleigh and smiling at me. Prince Praxatin was wearing a short
fur jacket and high boots, and I immediately noticed the scar
on his upper lip. It had been sewn badly and had healed badly.
What sort of wound had that been? It looked like the result of
a jab by a big bird.

"A good journey, doctor?" he said. "I sent you the big sleigh
because of the luggage, but I see you have only these two small
suitcases."

This man who was now slinking out of the room with a
broom under his arm spoke to me with friendly condescension,
as if to a subordinate. I naturally took him to be the owner of
the Morwede estate and rose to my feet.

"Have I the honour of addressing Baron von Malchin . . . ?"

"No, I'm not the baron, I'm only his estate manager," he
interrupted. "Prince Arkady Praxatin – yes, I'm a Russian, a

25

leaf torn from the tree by the gale, one of those typical *émigrés* who always tell the same story, in Russia they owned I don't know how many *desyatins*, as well as a palace in Petrograd and another in Moscow, and now they're waiters in some restaurant – except that I happen not to be a waiter, but to be earning a living here on this estate."

He was still holding my hand in his. Behind what he was now saying there was a gloomy indifference and a trace of the kind of self-irony that is embarrassing to a listener. I wanted to introduce myself, but he seemed to regard this as unnecessary and did not give me a chance to speak.

"Manager, agent, bailiff, what you will," he went on. "I might just as well have become the estate chef. Perhaps that's the field in which my talents really lie. At home my *piroshki*, my mushrooms in cream sauce, my game soups with individual meat pies were famous throughout the neighbourhood. Life was still worth living in those days. But here, in this country, this neighbourhood . . . Do you play cards, doctor? Baccarat, perhaps, or écarté? No? What a pity. This is a lonely waste, as you'll find out for yourself, there's no social life here."

At last he let my hand go, lit a cigarette and looked up dreamily at the evening sky and the pale moon while I shivered and covered myself with the rug. Then he went on with his monologue.

"Never mind the loneliness, it's all right with me. But life here is an ordeal. Sometimes when I dress in the morning I say to myself, you live this dreary life, but it's your own fault, you wanted it. That was when the Bolsheviks arrested me – not to my dying day shall I ever know why – I feared for my life, trembled with fear, prayed to God on my knees, I'm young, I said, take pity on me, I want to live. Go to the devil, God said to me, you're just the martyr to the faith I want, so go away and live. And this is the life I'm living. Others – they too sinned, piled up evil in their hearts, played and drank and squandered their gold and silver and wept far too little about their sins – and now they're actually happy, living like peasants, satisfied if they have a little moonshine to drink with their groats. They don't think. But I spend all my time thinking about myself, that's my illness, doctor, I think far too much. You don't sympathise with those Reds, do you, doctor?"

I told him I took no interest whatever in politics. He must have detected the irritation and impatience behind my answer, because he took a step backwards, struck his brow with his hand, and began reproaching himself.

"Here I am, standing about and talking, actually talking politics, while there's a sick child in the house – what will you think of me, doctor? The baron, my friend and benefactor, said to me: 'Arkady Fyodorovich, go and meet the doctor and, unless he's exhausted by the journey, ask him to stop off on the way and see a patient, a little girl here in the forester's lodge. She has been feverish for two days. It may be scarlet fever.'"

I got out of the sleigh and followed him into the house. Meanwhile the coachman unhitched the horses to allow them to move. A young fox emerged from the kennel in which it was chained and howled at us furiously. The Russian aimed a kick and shook his fist at it.

"Quiet, you thrice damned fiendish bastard, get back into your hole," he shouted at it. "You've seen me often enough, you ought to know me by now, but you still don't, you useless beast, you're not worth the food you eat."

We went into the house. A poorly lit corridor led to a dark, unheated room in which I could see practically nothing, and knocked my shin painfully against the edge of a chair. "Straight on, doctor," the Russian said, but I stopped and listened to a violin being played in the next room.

It was a melancholy tune that forms the first bars of a Tartini sonata in which ghosts flicker, and it grips me whenever I hear it. A childhood memory of mine is associated with it. I'm in my father's house, everyone has gone out and left me alone. It's getting dark, everything's quiet, only the wind whistles quietly in the chimney, and I'm afraid, because everything all

27

round is bewitched, and I'm full of the childish fear of being alone, and of tomorrow, and of life itself.

For a moment I stood there like a small, frightened boy close to tears. Then I pulled myself together. "Who plays the first movement of the sonata here in this lonely house?" I asked. As if he had been reading my thoughts the Russian answered:

"That's Federico. I thought I'd find him here. He hasn't been seen since early morning. Instead of staying at home and doing his French, he's here playing the fiddle. Come along, doctor."

The violin playing stopped when we went into the room. A middle-aged woman with pale cheeks, who looked as if she had been up all night, rose from the foot of the bed and looked at me with anxious, expectant eyes. The dimmed light of a petrol lamp fell on the quilted bedcover and the pillows and the thin face of the little patient, who must have been thirteen or fourteen. A blackened oak figure of Christ held its arms outstretched over the bed. The boy who had been playing the sonata sat motionless on the window ledge with his violin on his knees.

"Well?" said the Russian when I had finished examining the patient.

"You're right, it is scarlet fever," I replied. "I'll send a notification of infectious illness to the head of the district."

"The head of the district is the baron, and I keep his diary," the Russian said. "I'll fill in the form and send it to you for signature tomorrow."

While I washed my hands I gave the woman the necessary instructions for the night. To show that she would forget nothing of what I said she repeated it in a voice in which there was anxiety and tension; she did not take her eyes off the child for a moment. Meanwhile the Russian turned to the boy who was still sitting motionless on the window ledge.

"Now you see what an embarrassing position you've put me in, Federico," he said. "You're forbidden to come here, but you take no notice and come here every day, you hurry here as if driven by the wind. And the consequence of your

28

disobedience is that you're now in a sick-room and perhaps you've already caught the scarlet fever. What am I to do? I shall have to tell your father that I found you here."

The boy's voice came out of the darkness. "You won't do that, Arkady Fyodorovich," he said. "I know you won't do that."

"You know that? Are you quite sure of what you're saying. Are you actually threatening me, perhaps? What are you threatening me with? Federico, I'm talking to you absolutely seriously. What do you mean by what you have just said? Tell me."

The boy did not answer, and his silence seemed to worry the Russian. He took a step forward and went on: "You sit there in the dark just like an owl. You sit there threateningly and say nothing. Do you by any chance think you're frightening me? What have I to be frightened of? Certainly, I've often played cards with you, not for my own pleasure, but for your entertainment. And as for the paper you signed . . . ."

"I'm not talking about trente et quarante and I haven't threatened you," the boy said with a trace of pride and indignation in his voice. "You won't say anything, Arkady Fyodorovich, simply because you're a gentleman."

"So that's what you think," the Russian said after a moment's reflection. "Very well, let us assume that for your sake I once more behave like a gentleman and say nothing, that doesn't alter the fact that you'll be here again tomorrow."

"That's quite certain," the boy replied. "I'll be here tomorrow and every day."

The little girl's hand appeared from under the bed cover and she said quietly without opening her eyes: "Are you still there, Federico?"

The boy slid noiselessly from the window ledge.

"Yes, I'm still here, Elsie, I'm still here with you. And the doctor's here too, and you'll soon be well again and able to get up."

Meanwhile the Russian seemed to have made up his mind.

29

"It's impossible," he announced. "I can't let you go on with these visits. I can't take the responsibility in relation to your father . . ."

The boy cut him short with a gesture.

"You have no responsibility, Arkady Fyodorovich," he said. "I take full responsibility myself. You know nothing, you have never seen me here."

So far I had been more amused than irritated by the way the Russian negotiated with this adolescent, but now it seemed to me that it was time for me to intervene.

"Young man," I said, "the situation is not as simple as that. As a doctor I have something to say. By staying in this room you have become a carrier of the illness. You have become a danger to everyone with whom you come in contact. Do you understand that?"

The boy did not answer. He was standing in the dark and I felt his eyes on me.

"So," I said, "you will be isolated and under observation for two weeks. I shall see to that, and of course I shall have to inform your father."

"Are you being serious?" he said, and I noted with pleasure that his voice had changed and had lost some of its confidence.

"Of course," I said. "I'm dead tired and in no mood for joking."

"No, you mustn't tell my father," he said quietly but firmly. "For heaven's sake don't tell him you met me here."

"Unfortunately I have no choice in the matter," I said as calmly as I could. "I think we can go now, there's no more I can do here today. Besides, you don't strike me as having much spirit, young man. At your age I used to face a punishment I deserved with rather more courage."

For a while there was silence in the room. The only sound was the feverish child's quick breathing and the hiss of the petrol lamp.

"Arkady Fyodorovich, you're my friend," the boy said

30

suddenly. "Why don't you help me? You stand there and allow me to be insulted."

"You should not have said that, doctor," the Russian said. "You should not have said that, really. You must realise that he really is in a difficult situation. Our concern should be to help him. Don't you think it would be sufficient if we disinfected all his clothes and his underwear?"

"Yes, it might be," I admitted. "But you yourself heard the young gentleman say that he would be coming here again tomorrow and every day."

The boy was leaning against the window ledge, looking at me.

"And if I promise you not to come here again?" he said.

"Do you always change your mind so quickly?" I said. "What guarantee have I that you will keep your promise?"

Once more there was a silence, and then the Russian said: "You mustn't do Federico an injustice, doctor. You talk like that because you don't know him. I do. Actually I know him very well. If he gives his word, he keeps it, I vouch for that."

"Very well, then. He'll give me his word . . ."

"I'll give it to you, Arkady Fyodorovich," the boy interrupted me. "I'll give it to you, because you're my friend and a gentleman. I shall not come to this house as long as Elsie is ill. Will that do?"

The question was directed at the Russian, but I answered.

"Yes," I said.

The boy approached noiselessly, like a shadow.

"Can you hear me, Elsie?" he said. "I shan't be coming here again, I gave my word, you heard me," he said. "I had to. You know that if father finds out that I've been here with you he'll send me away from here, a long way away, perhaps even to strangers in the town. That's why it's better that I shouldn't come. Do you hear me, Elsie?"

"No, young gentleman, she can't hear you, she's asleep," the woman whispered.

She took the lamp and put it on the table. It now shone on the boy's face, and I saw it for the first time.

My first reaction was shock. If anyone, the Russian, for instance, had asked me a question I should not have been able to answer.

I felt pressure round my heart, I dropped my thermometer, my knees trembled, and I clutched the back of a chair for support.

After the bewilderment of the first few moments, when I was able to think more calmly again, I told myself it must have been an optical illusion. My nerves were on edge, my senses must have deceived me, my memory must have played a trick on me. The boy's face must have been covered up by the memory of another face that had haunted me all day long. A troublesome obsession that I must get rid of quickly.

The boy bent down, picked up the thermometer, and handed it to me. His face was now turned towards me and I saw it in a different light, and seeing it for a second time like this left no possible doubt in my mind that what I had seen was no illusion. Incredibly, the boy's features were those of the Gothic marble relief I had seen a few hours before among a lot of other junk in an antique dealer's window in Osnabrück.

What took me aback was not so much the external resemblance as the facial expression, which in both cases was the same. There was the same extraordinary juxtaposition of unbridled violence and dignified charm that had astonished me in the marble relief. True, the nose and chin were different: they were gentler and less sharply defined. It seemed to me that a person who had these features would be capable both of the wildest and gentlest impulses. The only new and surprising thing about this face was the big, blue eyes, which were full of silvery reflections, like irises.

By an effort of will I had been able to drag myself away from the marble relief in the shop window, but here I went on gazing at that face and those eyes as if under a spell. My behaviour was absurd, perhaps, but neither the boy nor the Russian seemed to notice what was happening inside me. The Russian stifled a yawn and said: "Are you ready, doctor? Shall we go?"

Without waiting for an answer, he turned to Federico and said: "The sleigh's outside. The big sleigh. There's room for more than three, so you can come with us, Federico."

"Thank you, but I'd rather go on foot, I know a short cut," the boy replied.

"You know the way only too well. Only too well," the Russian said teasingly. "I've no fear of *your* losing your way."

The boy did not answer. With his violin case under his arm he went over to the bed and looked at the sleeping child. Then he took his cap and coat and nodded at me as he walked past me and out.

"You offended him, doctor," the Russian said as the sleigh moved off. "You did it deliberately, I saw your eyes flash. You've made an enemy of him. It's bad to have made an enemy of Federico."

We left the wood and were driving in the dark across snow-covered fields, and the wind sang its sad tunes in the telegraph wires.

"Who is Federico's father?" I asked.

"His father? His real father is a small artisan somewhere in northern Italy. Federico comes from very humble circumstances. But the baron adopted him, and perhaps loves him even more than his own child."

"So he has a child of his own?"

The Russian was rather surprised. "Yes," he replied. "Your little patient, doctor. The child in the forester's lodge. Didn't I mention that your patient was the baron's little girl?"

"No, you didn't. But why does he let his child be looked after by others?"

I realised that I had no right to ask such a question.

"I beg your pardon, I didn't ask that question out of idle curiosity, but as a doctor," I said.

The Russian produced a box of matches from his fur coat

and tried to light his cigarette. This took some time. Eventually he replied: "Perhaps the forest air is better for the child's health. It's always misty in the village. The mist hangs about right through the autumn and winter. Look."

He pointed with his hand that was holding the cigarette to the scattered village lights, which seemed to be shining out of a thick, milky-white veil.

"It creeps into the village from the moor and the damp meadows. It's always there, day after day and night after night. It's even worse than the loneliness, it causes the gloomiest thoughts, it makes the soul sick. Perhaps you really ought to learn to play cards, doctor."

SIX

The house I lodged in belonged to the village tailor, a tall, thin man with blood-shot eyes and sluggish limbs. He had served with the Dragoons at Osnabrück, became an NCO in the Great War, and was wounded in the advance on Warsaw. His first wife had died of "chest trouble", and his second wife had contributed the house as well as some money to the marriage. He told me all this slowly and solemnly on the first evening, while helping me to unpack my instruments. Later I saw him only rarely, as he was always in his workshop. In my bedroom I sometimes heard him chopping firewood in the yard.

I saw his wife every day. She cleaned my rooms, looked after my clothes and did my washing. At first she cooked for me too, but later I preferred having my meals sent over from the inn. She was a quiet, hard worker and did not talk very much. On Sundays she wore a black skirt with yellow hem and yellow silk ribbons on the apron and a blue kerchief round her neck – a costume I saw nowhere else in the village and only once elsewhere in the neighbourhood.

I took an instant dislike to the old-fashioned furniture and fittings of my three rooms. The furniture and the ornaments were either useless or uncomfortable, and it was clear to me that I would not be able to live with them for long. In retrospect my feelings about them are more tolerant, and now I think quite warmly about my sitting and consulting room, with its framed photogravures, antlers, the two wicker chairs laden with cushions, the figure of a female water-carrier on the mantelpiece, and the wretched, dusty artificial flowers in the bedroom. They witnessed a great happiness, and I shall never see them again.

The first visitor to sit on one of the two wicker chairs was the village schoolmaster.

I had seen him from my window walking up and down outside the front door, unable to make up his mind to come in. Several times he looked as if he were about to do so, but then went away again. Then he came in, just when I was standing in front of the mirror, shaving. His face was thin and wrinkled, his greying hair had been allowed to grow long and had been cut in a "genius" style, a certainly deliberate untidiness about his dress was intended to indicate that he was above caring about appearances, and in fact he succeeded in looking rather like what one expects an itinerant teacher of elocution to look like.

He assured me immediately that he had come, not as a patient, but as a result of his healthy mistrust of his fellow-men. He had made it a matter of principle never to accept at second-hand the impressions of others, but to rely exclusively on his own personal, first-hand impressions. He did not allow himself to be influenced by others, for the chief activity of those "others", both here and elsewhere, consisted in trying to cause dissension between those who were to some extent dependent on each other and – at this point he paused briefly – perhaps meant something to each other.

Sitting in his wicker chair, he gazed reflectively at the fire while melted snow dripped from his boots and formed little rivulets and puddles on the floor.

He explained that in certain circles he enjoyed the reputation of being an uncongenial person, and he had made himself unpopular in higher circles in particular – he indicated the latter by a vague gesture in the direction of the top of the window. But he put up gladly with this unpopularity, which was the result of his natural propensity to total honesty, his principle of always telling the truth and nothing but the truth. He always spoke his mind and called things by their proper name – in that respect he made no concessions, even to the higher ups. This candour was of course unwelcome to certain persons, particularly those who had something to hide, but he, the schoolmaster, could not have any consideration for them.

He changed the subject.

"The neighbourhood's very unhealthy," he declared, "and, so far as hygiene is concerned, we are backward in every respect, the whole atmosphere is reactionary and hostile to progress. So you'll find there's plenty of work for you to do here. Your predecessor would gladly have had a more restful time, at any rate in his last years, but that was not granted him. He was seventy-two when he died. I can say that I found real friendship in this house. He and I agreed on everything, in general and in particular. How many evenings have I spent in this room in friendly conversation over bread and butter and a bottle of beer."

He pointed to a photogravure showing a Shakespearean-looking king seated on his throne while two women flung themselves at his feet appealing for his aid, and an exotic-looking ambassador with his retinue, complete with horses and camels, waited in the background.

"That was my last Christmas present," he explained. "It gave the old gentleman a great deal of pleasure, and he gave it a place of honour. Now it belongs to the local authority, which bought all his goods and chattels at auction. The whole thing was not quite above board, of course, and certain persons made themselves quite a pile on the sly, but they shouldn't count their blessings too soon, because they're known, and the last word on the matter has not yet been spoken."

He sat for a while in silent contemplation of the picture. When I told him I was about to call on the owner of the estate he offered to come with me to show me the way. If I had gone by myself I could not have missed it, for the big, two-storey building of red sandstone with a steep blue roof was visible from the village street behind a group of leafless, snow-covered beech trees.

37

On the way the conversation turned to my landlord and his first wife.

"What did he tell you?" he asked. "Did he say she was dead? Of chest trouble? It takes a long time to die of that. She's alive and kicking, she went off with the agent of an artificial fertiliser factory. Dead? Is that what he said? Appeared before her Maker? There you have it. She's as healthy as you or I. To vouch for it I'd lay my head on the block."

I told him there was no need to do anything so uncomfortable for my sake, as it was all the same to me whether the woman was alive or dead. But he had worked himself up to such a pitch of indignation that he had to tell me the whole story.

"And his present wife betrays him too, except that her lover is here in the village. The first one was the blacksmith's elder son, but now it's the younger one's turn. The tailor gets his own back by stealing the money from the money box and spending it on brandy. The whole place is rotten to the core. Even the butter still in the milk is rancid."

He said goodbye near the well in front of the small lawn in the park, where the rose trees sheltered behind their protective covering of straw.

"You're too easily taken in," he said to me in a tone of slight disapproval. "They'll soon find out they can cheat you right and left. If you want to find out the truth about anyone here, you have only to ask me. I know them all, may the Lord have pity on me."

Then he made off down the drive by which we had come, and as he went he struck at the red berries of the gorse bushes with his walking stick. The wind blew open his thin overcoat, and he looked as if he were carrying all his pitiful knowledge of his fellow villagers in a big brown bag on his bent back. At the park gate he turned once more and raised his green felt hat to me in an expansive gesture of farewell.

SEVEN

Baron von Malchin received me in his study, a big, low, oak-panelled room looking out on to a terrace and the park. Thick clouds of cigar smoke lingered over the desk, clung to the bookshelves, and dispersed after mounting to the worm-eaten beams that supported the ceiling. On the walls there was a collection of old cutting and thrusting weapons, among which I noticed a number of rare and awe-inspiring items. I spotted a sixtenth-century mace, a Polish battle-axe, the handle of which was wrapped in leather straps, a Swiss partisan, a Spanish mace, a sixteenth-century hunting spear, a fifteenth-century *martel de fer*, a huge two-handed sword, and a *schiavona*, a type of Venetian sword. The two-handed sword seemed to be of Saracen origin and I gazed at it admiringly while talking to the baron about his daughter's condition.

He listened attentively, and I concluded from the little that he said that he had gone to see the child early that morning, and that the forester's wife was an experienced nurse and had brought up two children of her own who had been sickly from birth.

"My little Elsie is in good hands, and now that you're here my mind is completely at rest," he said.

That was all that was said about little Elsie on this occasion. The baron changed the subject and started talking about my father.

When I think of my father I generally see him busy with his work. Not till I began to think and observe my environment did I develop any clear ideas about his work. At that early age there was no doubt in my mind that the sheets of paper covered with small and delicate handwriting that lay on his desk consisted of prayers and magic spells that protected the house from thieves. I admired my father, and his work filled me with awe and curiosity. Later I found out from our housekeeper that what he was doing was writing history, that I must not disturb him while he was so engaged, and that what he wrote had nothing to do with the stories of adventure by land and sea that I borrowed from the lending library, saw in the hands of my school-fellows, and found among my presents at Christmas time. That made me lose interest in my father's work for a long time.

I have distinct memories of him in his last years. I see him walking up and down the room with lowered head, lost in thought, or checking our elderly housekeeper's accounts. He always looked pale and rather tired, and his furrowed brow suggested the worries of which he often spoke, and perhaps also grief and sometimes disappointment. I remember him as a very lonely man who lived only for me and for his work.

But that picture in no way coincided with that drawn for me by the baron. His was perhaps a youthful portrait of a man I got to know only in his declining years. The baron knew him as an attractive man of the world who captivated women and enchanted men, a wine-lover who enjoyed shooting, a guest welcome at noble houses everywhere, who gave himself freely and was lavish with valuable ideas over a bottle of wine and a cigar. That was how my father, whose last, tired years I had seen, lived in Baron von Malchin's memory.

"That is amazing," I said quietly, lost in thought.

"Yes. He was a man of remarkable gifts," the baron went on. "I often think of him. He really was a man of great personality. What would I give to be able to talk to him again and thank him."

"Thank him?" I said in surprise. "What for?"

An answer I had not expected came from a cloud of cigar smoke.

"I have more to thank him for than he himself suspected," the baron said. "He died too soon. My life's work developed out of an idea that he casually mentioned."

"So your subject is German mediaeval history?"

The baron looked at me. The friendly expression on his narrow, sharply outlined face gave way to a hard, passionate, fanatical look.

"I have given up historical research," he said. "I'm now working in the scientific field."

He looked at me searchingly once more. Perhaps he was looking for my father's features in my face. I said nothing, and looked at the mediaeval weapons hanging on the walls.

"My little collection seems to interest you," he said, resuming his friendly and slightly impersonal expression. "That two-handed sword seems to fascinate you."

"Saracen, late twelfth century, isn't it?"

"Quite right. I have another item from the same workshop, a coat of mail. The sword's name is cut into the blade, it's Al Rosub, the blade that cuts deep. It was used in the battles of the Second Crusade, its last owner died at Benevento at the same time as his master, Manfred, the Emperor's son."

He pointed to a short, curved sword, shaped like a sabre, that hung under the Saracen blade.

"And do you know what that is?"

I replied that that kind of weapon was known in France as a *braquemart* and Germany as a *malchus*. The shape was very ancient. The hunting knives with which Roman gladiators were armed looked very much like it.

"Excellent," the baron exclaimed. "I see that you're a connoisseur. You must come and see me often, doctor, whenever you have time. No, really, doctor, you must promise to do that. The evenings are long, and you won't find much company here."

He rose and fetched glasses and a bottle of whisky, and while pacing up and down the room enumerated the persons in the neighbourhood who in his opinion were possible company for me.

"There's my old friend, the priest, for instance," he said. "He confirmed me. You'll be surprised, doctor, at the extent of that simple country priest's knowledge. He's a thoroughly good and decent person. Only – don't misunderstand me, doctor – the last few years have made him rather tired. Talking to him has lost some of its former charm. Another whisky, doctor? It's not good to stand on one leg. He looks at the things of this world with an indulgence that is misinterpreted by some people. It's certainly not simplicity, good gracious no, it may be only resignation. My old friend takes his years badly."

He threw away the stub of his cigar and went on: "You know my manager, Prince Praxatin, don't you? He can teach you every conceivable card game, besides instructing you in the Russian way of looking at life. Incidentally, he's the last of the line of Rurik. Yes, the Praxatins are descended from the Ruriks. If the world were not ruled by injustice, today he'd be seated on the throne of the Tsars."

"Or have been shot dead in a lead mine in the Urals," I remarked.

Baron von Malchin stopped right in front of me and looked at me challengingly.

"You think so? I take the liberty of thinking otherwise. Don't forget that the Holstein-Gottorps were strangers in the country and remained strangers, even when they adopted the name of Romanov. Under their legitimate ruling house the Russian people would have developed on different lines."

He resumed his walk round the room.

"You'll meet my assistant in a week's time. I sent her to Berlin yesterday with my car. We need a more effective high-pressure steriliser."

"For agricultural purposes?" I asked, but merely out of politeness, for I had not the slightest interest in why a high-pressure steriliser was needed on Baron von Malchin's estate.

"No," the baron replied. "It's not for agricultural purposes.

I'm trying to solve a quite specific scientific problem, as I mentioned to you. The young lady who is helping me with the work is a bacteriologist and doctor of chemistry."

I had been listening with little interest, it was all the same to me what sort of problem the baron was tackling, and whether it was scientific or not was no concern of mine, but at these last words of his the possibility of an extraordinary coincidence flashed through my mind, a fierce joy accompanied by a terror of disappointment – I did not dare to believe in the impossible – a bacteriologist – Bibiche – a doctor of chemistry – the baron had sent his assistant to Berlin the day before, when I had seen Bibiche in the station square at Osnabrück – she would be coming back in a week's time – it was impossible that she should be living here, quite close, that I should be able to see her every day – such miracles did not happen, it was a dream – he had sent her to Berlin in his car – in a green Cadillac, perhaps? – I must ask him, ask him immediately.

But the baron had gone back to what he had been talking about before.

"And there's also the schoolmaster, of course. I don't much want to talk about him, I'd rather leave you to form your own opinion. Or have you already met him, perhaps? You have? Then you know all about him already. He calls himself a free-thinker – and what sort of freedom is that? He has the wickedest tongue in the whole place, he hasn't a good word for anyone and sees intrigues everywhere – he sees through people, doesn't he? You can't pull wool over his eyes, can you? I don't know why, but he believes me to be his sworn enemy, and there's nothing I can do about it. All the same, he's basically harmless. People here know him and let him talk."

Meanwhile I had calmed down again. I had been thinking it over. It was impossible that Bibiche should be living here in this village. She was spoilt, courted, needed luxury and the facilities and conveniences of a big city, she could not live

43

without them. How absurd to expect to find her here, among these smoke-blackened peasants' houses and snow-covered potato fields and the puddles of this muddy village street. I had given up the idea of finding her here.

Nevertheless something impelled me to ask the baron about his car, the car in which his assistant had driven to Berlin. I did so obliquely.

"Perhaps I shall be called out to patients in the surrounding area from time to time," I said. "Is there a car in the village I could use in emergencies?"

The baron emptied his glass of whisky. Smoke rose from his cigar, which he had put in the ashtray.

"I have a car myself," the baron said. "I hardly ever use it, of course. I'm the nearly extinct type of person who isn't in a hurry and prefers a saddle to a driving seat. I don't like this mechanical age very much. In the fields here – incidentally, it's good soil, doctor, lime, marshland, sandy heath, and then marly soil again – on my estate you'll see no tractors or seeding machines and nothing but horses and the plough. And in the barns in late summer you'll hear the ancient song of the threshing flail. So it was in my grandfather's time, and so it will remain as long as I live."

He picked up his cigar and thoughtfully wiped away the ash on the table. He seemed to have forgotten that I had asked about his car.

"My dead sister," he went on, "had electric light put in every room in the house. I prefer working by the light of an oil lamp. You smile, doctor? The really great masterpieces were composed in the light of oil lamps, Virgil's *Aeneid* and Goethe's *Faust* alike. They shone on the unknown master who designed Aachen Cathedral on a crude peasant's table. Christ was familiar with their mild and friendly light, and the Wise Virgins in the Bible carried them when they went to meet the Saviour – but what were we talking about? You can take my car whenever you need it, doctor. It's an eight-cylinder tourer, a Cadillac, I . . . . Don't you feel well, doctor? Some brandy?

44

A glass of water? Good gracious, how dreadful you look. Do you feel better now? Thank goodness. You're as white as a sheet, doctor."

EIGHT

The sudden surge of surprise and delight, the disappearance of the tension inside me, the excitement I wanted to conceal though it was beyond my power to suppress – the only explanation I can think of for all this is that it must have resulted in a remarkable split taking place in my consciousness. I heard the baron's voice, I heard every word he said, but at the same time I felt I was no longer there, but in bed in a sick-room somewhere. I felt this quite distinctly: there was a warm, damp something on my brow and at the back of my head. I tried to touch it, but suddenly I could not move my arm, and I heard the nurse's soft footsteps. That seems to have been my first premonition of the state in which the whole of this adventure was to end for me. Later I had such premonitions several times, but usually only when I was tired, generally at night when I was just dropping off to sleep, but never so vividly as that morning. I wondered what was the matter with me. Where am I? I said to myself. A moment ago I was talking to the baron. Bibiche is coming, she'll be here in a week's time. Then I came round. The baron was bending over me with a glass of brandy in his hand. I emptied it, and then emptied it a second time. What happened to me? I wondered. Was I dreaming? Yes, dreaming in broad daylight. Bibiche is coming, that isn't a dream, it's reality. Aloud I said something about overwork and slight attacks of faintness that didn't mean anything.

"That's a city-dweller's nerves," I heard the baron saying. "Life in the country will be good for you." The words "life in the country" reminded me of Bibiche, and I realised I had made an enormous emotional leap. A few moments before I had not dared hope I should ever see her again, and now a whole week's wait before seeing her struck me as nearly intolerable.

By now I had my nerves under control again, and felt rather ashamed of what had happened. "The air's bad in here," the baron said. "Let us let some ozone in. I've been smoking like a chimney all morning." He rose and opened a window. A gust of cold air swept through the room, the papers on the desk rustled, and at that moment Federico must have come in. When I caught sight of him he was standing against the oak panelling between the two-handed sword and a Scottish claymore. He must have come straight from the moor or the forest, for snow mingled with pine needles was on his leggings and the shiny bluish head of some marsh bird protruded from his open game bag. Once more I was amazed at the resemblance – no, it was not an illusion, this boy had the features, the noble features of a man long dead who must have been a great man in his time – and when I saw him standing next to the two-handed sword I had a strange thought. He was born for that weapon, I said to myself, it was made for him. And I was almost surprised to see that instead of the sword he was holding a shot-gun.

A smile flitted across the baron's hard, narrow face.

"Back already?" he said. "I didn't expect to see you before midday. How's the work in the forest going?"

"The tree-fellers have nearly got down to the stream. Carting the stuff away is going to begin tomorrow. Two new men, railway workers, have been taken on."

"I don't much like railway workers," the baron said. "They're no good. Who took them on? Praxatin?"

He turned to me without waiting for an answer.

"This is Federico," he said, without mentioning anything else, neither the lad's origin or the relationship between them. "And this is our new doctor, he arrived yesterday."

Federico bowed slightly, and nothing in his face betrayed that we had already met. I took a step towards him, but the

47

surprise and rejection in his iris-blue eyes reminded me that we were enemies, and I dropped my half-outstretched hand and stopped. The baron noticed nothing.

"Do you shoot?" he said. "Federico knows every hare for miles around. The shooting's good here, even roe-deer can be seen from time to time. You know nothing about shooting? What a pity. Your father used to bring down the duck in droves, doctor. I'll teach you stalking if you like. You don't want to? I'm sorry to hear it. Don't you go in for any kind of sport?"

"I do. I fence."

"Oh, do you? That interests me. German? Italian?"

I told him I was equally practised in both schools.

This piece of information delighted him.

"We've certainly scored a hit with you," he exclaimed. "It's so rare to come across a good fencer. What do you say to a short bout?"

"Now?"

"If it suits you."

"Certainly. With pleasure. With you?"

"No, with Federico. He's my pupil, and a very gifted pupil, if I may say so. But perhaps you're still tired. That little faint just now . . ."

I glanced at Federico. He was waiting for my answer with an expression of tense excitement. When he noticed I was looking at him he turned away.

"That's all over," I said to the baron. "I feel perfectly fit now, and I'm at your service."

"Splendid," said the baron. "Federico, take the doctor to the gym. Here's the key to the sword cupboard. I'll come along later."

Federico went ahead, humming an Italian tune. He walked so quickly that I had difficulty keeping up. In the gym we took off our jackets and waistcoats, and he silently handed me the head mask and foil. Obviously he had no intention of waiting for the baron. We stood apart and saluted each other, and then took up our positions.

48

Federico began with a lunge from quarte and a one-two followed by a cut-over in regular text-book fashion which I had no difficulty in parrying. Actually, I did not expect much pleasure from this bout, I had accepted the challenge only to please the baron. My heart was not in it, but I felt quite sure of myself, and while mechanically parrying my opponent's thrusts and lunges my mind was on Bibiche, whom I was soon going to see again.

But then the bout took a turn that I had not expected. After a beat by which I displaced his blade Federico replied with a series of feints which he carried out very skilfully indeed. I suddenly realised that I had underrated him, and before I was able to guess his intentions a riposte came out of his circular parry that I was only half able to parry. It touched my shoulder.

"Touché," I called out, and resumed my stance. I was furious with myself, and could not understand how I had allowed this to happen. In the past few years I had won prizes at two tournaments, and here I was up against a novice, an adolescent.

"Well, that's that," I said, and at the same time noticed that my shirt was torn over the left shoulder and that blood was coming from a small scratch, and only now did I realise that the point of my opponent's foil lacked the leather-covered button that is supposed to prevent wounds. He had been using a deadly weapon.

He had taken off his mask.

"There's no safety-button on your foil," I pointed out. "Did you know that?"

"The same applies to yours," he replied.

For a moment I did not realise what he meant. I looked at him in surprise, but he withstood my gaze.

You don't expect me to fight a duel with a schoolboy?

No, I didn't say that, I only wanted to. But the look in those big, silvery blue iris eyes prevented me, and then something happened inside me that to the present day I do not understand. Perhaps it was anger at having been pinked, perhaps it was the desire to get my own back, to make good the indignity I had suffered. But no, it cannot have been that alone, it was his eyes, the expression on that strange face of his that held me under its spell, made me feel suddenly that I was faced not with a boy, but a man – a man whom I had offended and to whom I owed satisfaction.

I heard Federico's voice.

"Well? Are you ready?" he said.

I forgot all my hesitations and felt nothing but an ardent desire to deal with this opponent.

"Come on," I called out, and our foils crossed.

At first I had a kind of plan, I remember. I still believed I was his superior and that the outcome of the encounter was in my hands. I did not want to wound him, but to restrict myself to defence, to parry his attacks and, when the opportunity arose, to knock the weapon from his hand.

That is not what happened.

After the first few thrusts and parries I realised that so far he had been only playing with me. Now he was in earnest. I was faced with a fencer of stature and a bitter enemy. He attacked me with a boldness and a passion and at the same time with a cautiousness that I had never before met in an opponent. With whom was I fencing? I wondered as I retreated step by step. Who is this terrible opponent? Whence this ungovernable spirit? I had no more thought of restricting myself to defence, I realised that I was fighting for my life, and I attacked, but he parried my onslaughts with ease. I was startled to discover that this was an opponent against whom I had no chance. He had driven me back to the wall. My arm was tiring and I felt that I was lost. I knew that the last decisive thrust was coming in the next few moments, and with the strength of despair I tried to postpone the inevitable. I was afraid . . .

A voice called out "Stop."

We stopped.

"Well, doctor," the baron asked, "are you satisfied with my pupil?"

I think I laughed. My answer was a hysterical laugh.

"I shall now take charge, Federico, do as I say. Take a step back. And another. Hits to be acknowledged. Are you ready? Go."

His orders followed in rapid succession, and so did Federico's responses.

"Balestra! Parry! Disengage! Quarte! Well done, doctor. Riposte! Bind! Good. Disarm him!"

The weapon flew from my hand. Federico picked it up and handed it to me. Then he silently offered me his hand.

The baron accompanied me to the park gate, where he said goodbye.

"He fences pretty well for a fifteen-year-old, doesn't he?" he said.

"Fifteen, is he?" I repeated. "But he's not a boy, he's a man."

The baron dropped my hand.

"Quite right, so he is," he replied, and a shadow flitted across his face. "The people from whom he comes mature before their time."

On the way back to my lodgings I was in a strange frame of mind. I felt, not as if I were walking, but as if I were floating down the village street – sometimes one feels like that in a dream, as if one were gliding along on a breath of wind. I felt weightless, and at the same time deeply moved. Bibiche was coming, and I had just fought a duel, a matter of life and death. My whole being was stirred up, I felt far more than usual that I was alive.

I think I was very happy that morning.

A little old woman was in my waiting room, the mother of the shopkeeper next door. She complained of a painful cough, shortness of breath, difficulty in swallowing and a bad sore throat.

I looked at her in uncomprehending surprise.

I had completely forgotten that I was the village doctor.

NINE

I met her, I met Bibiche a week later, it was about midday, dogs were scuffling in the village street and the shopkeeper standing outstide his shop door called out to me that a thaw was coming. I went on, turned the corner, and saw the green Cadillac. It was standing in front of a small, friendly-looking house with blue-painted shutters and a bow-window-like structure projecting over the front door. Two men from the estate farm had lifted a big, irregularly shaped object covered in sailcloth and were carrying it into the entrance hall. Bibiche was standing near them talking to Prince Praxatin. She did not see me. A brown German shepherd dog was rubbing its head against her black sealskin fur, and sparrows chattered noisily in the winter sun all around her.

"So you found him," the Russian was saying. "You actually spoke to him. What an angel you are, Kallisto. Your words ring in my ear like the bells at the holy festival of Easter. How is he? What is he doing? Is his head still full of plans? If he has a hundred roubles in his pocket, he'll be turning them into thousands, that's the kind of man he is. But why hasn't he answered my letters? Is he ashamed of past times and his old friend?"

Bibiche answered, and for the first time for an age I heard her dark, silky-soft voice.

"What a lot of questions," she said. "No, he didn't get your letters. He has changed his job three times in the last year. For a time he had nowhere to live, he just wandered the streets. Until a month ago he was a watchmaker's assistant."

"He was always mechanically gifted, he even invented things," said the Russian. "And what is he doing now?"

"In the daytime your friend sells newspapers, and in the evening he puts on livery and stands outside the City of Cologne Restaurant and helps customers into their cars."

"My friend?" the Russian exclaimed. "Does he say we were friends? We were never friends. I knew him, and we used to play cards at the club. And how much does he earn? Did he tell you?"

"On good days he may earn about eight marks."

"Eight marks. He's on his own and has no one to worry about. He can live splendidly on five marks and even treat himself to a schnapps at lunch time. That leaves him with three marks a day, that's ninety marks a month and at the end of the year – nothing at all, it doesn't even add up to the interest on what he owes me. I spit at it – *passez moi l'expression.* Did he mention his debt?"

"No, he probably forgot about it long ago."

"Forgot?" the prince exclaimed. "A gaming debt? A debt of honour? Seventy thousand roubles, gold roubles in cash, payable within a week. Forget it, did you say? Well, I'll write and remind him. One day I'll get the money. He'll be rich again, I know. A man like him doesn't remain a newspaper seller for long. A man like him . . . Will you be quiet. Lie down."

These last words were meant for the German shepherd dog, which had suddenly jumped up and tried to chase the sparrows. Bibiche bent down and stroked it, and it put its muzzle in her hand.

"You must forgive me if I leave you now," said the prince. "I have all sorts of correspondence to deal with, and a lot of letters to write before lunch. Once more, thank you."

He turned and saw me standing behind the car.

"There's our doctor," he exclaimed. "Off to lunch already? Kallisto, allow me to introduce Dr Amberg . . ."

"That's quite unnecessary, we know each other already," she said. "That is, I don't know . . ."

She waved to Prince Praxatin, who had got into the car and was taking it back to the garage. Then she turned to me.

"I'm not sure if you remember me," she said.

"If I remember you? Your name is Kallisto Tsanaris, and you worked in front of the second window on the right. When you first arrived you wore a smooth, cornflower-blue dress with a blue and white striped shawl . . ."

"Quite right," she interrupted me.

"After that you never wore that dress again. Once, in November, you stayed away for eleven days. Were you ill? When you talked to yourself, you called yourself Bibiche, and you smoked small, thin, cork-tipped cigarettes . . ."

"Really – you still remember all that? So perhaps I made a small impression on you after all. But in that case I don't understand why you took not the slightest notice of me the whole time I was there. I confess to you that I took a great deal of trouble to make you notice me, but you seemed determined to ignore me. Unfortunately, I nearly said."

I looked at her. Why had she said that? It wasn't true, after all.

"Admit," she went on, "that for six months we worked in the same room and all you said to me was good morning and good night. Admit you were a bit proud and rather moody, perhaps you had been spoiled by too many beautiful women. The little Greek student didn't exist for you."

I began to consider. Might there be some truth in what she was saying? Might the fault have been really mine? Had I been too diffident, too timid, too cowardly – perhaps even too proud?

"Are you sorry?" she asked casually. "Well, it still isn't too late, as you see. Chance has brought us both here. Perhaps we may yet be friends after all. Eh?"

With some hesitation and an uncertain smile, she held out her hand. I took it, and didn't let it go. I couldn't speak. I felt like a man confronted with something contrary to the laws of nature, who had seen a miracle with his own eyes.

"Yes," she added thoughtfully. "That blue dress. I gave it to my maid."

Suddenly she began to laugh.

"Did you hear what he said? Prince Praxatin and his seventy thousand roubles? Did you understand what it was all about? You didn't? Well, I'll explain."

She leant slightly against me, and her arm touched mine.

"The fact is," she went on, "that he lost nothing in the Revolution. He had gambled away everything he had even before the war. He used to play every evening, he was a gambling addict. One evening he played poker at the club with three young gentlemen, sons of big industrialists and landowners. That evening for the first time in his life he had luck, fairy-tale luck, he won 240,000 roubles. His partners were the sons of immensely rich men, and all this is as good as cash in the bank, he said to himself as he picked up the IOUs. But next day the storming of the Winter Palace, the October Revolution took place, and after that who gave a moment's thought to gambling debts? The Revolution deprived those three young men of every penny they possessed, and now they're *émigrés*, struggling to make a living from one day to the next. But every month Prince Praxatin writes a letter to each of them, a very polite letter, reminding them of their debt and asking whether they are yet in a position to pay off their IOUs. One of them is a woodworker in Jugoslavia, another teaches languages in London, and the third sells newspapers in Berlin. Actually it's not so funny, sometimes I feel sorry for the prince."

"Why are you sorry for him?" I said. "He's happy. He lives in a dream, and so his wealth is more secure than any other. Because what one possesses in a dream cannot be taken away by a world of enemies. Only the awakening – but who would be cruel enough to wake him from his dream?"

"What one possesses in a dream cannot be taken away by a world of enemies," she repeated quietly. "That's very beautiful what you've just said."

We were silent for a while. It had grown cold, grey clouds had obscured the sun, mist in thick waves crept along the village street like a great, clumsy animal swallowing up roofs, windows, doors and fences.

"It's late," she said suddenly. "It's two o'clock. I must change, I've just come from Berlin, and the baron expects me at three."

She pointed at the blue shutters.

"I work there," she said. "That's the laboratory. As you see, it's not difficult to find me. And if I'm not here, I'm at the baron's in the manor house. We'll see each other soon, shan't we?"

She waved to me and was gone.

I should have been happy, I should have been glad. But when I was alone I had an agonising thought.

I played with it. At first I played with it as if it were a game.

All this – I said to myself – was as beautiful and as fleeting as a dream. As if it were a dream, I repeated. And I began to think how small the difference was between past reality and dreaming. But supposing it was really a dream. I stopped. Perhaps I'm still dreaming, I said to myself. I'm dreaming all this, the snow in the village street, the crow on the tree over there, the mist, the houses, the pale sun in the winter sky. And soon I shall wake up and it will all have disappeared, I'm going to wake up now, this very moment . . .

It was an absurd game that I played with myself, but I grew frightened and began to run. There was a shriek of not yet, not yet, inside me, but then I was back at my lodgings, the stairs creaked beneath my feet, I opened the door and was met by the familiar faint smell of chloroform that never left my room and did me good and drove away the craziest ideas.

TEN

My neighbour the shopkeeper who had called out to me that a thaw was on the way was a bad forecaster. Next day, instead of a thaw, bitterly cold rain fell. The rain was interspersed with watery snowflakes, and it went on falling for hours. When I got back from the forester's lodge at about ten a.m. I was frozen to the marrow.

I stopped the sleigh in front of the inn, went into the bar and ordered a brandy to warm myself. To my surprise the baron was there, discussing the falling price of cattle and the decline in the consumption of beer with the landlord. When he saw me he joined me immediately.

"I was just coming to see you, doctor," he said. "I called at your place an hour ago, but I was told you were out. You've been to the forester's lodge? Well, how is your little patient? Come along doctor, I'll come with you."

While we crossed the road I told him what he wanted to know. Little Elsie's condition was satisfactory. The fever had subsided, the throat was better, and the rash was beginning to disappear.

"Already?" said the baron. "Yes, for the past year or so scarlet fever in this part of the world has been appearing in a noticeably milder form. I assure you, doctor, I have not been anxious about the girl for a single moment."

There was nothing new about that, I knew it already.

The patients sitting on the bench in my waiting room rose when we walked in. There were three of them, two men and a woman. The baron looked them over and came with me into my consulting room.

"Busy?" he asked after he had sat down and lit his cigar.

"Not bad," I replied. "At the moment the patients are only from the village. Outside it they don't yet know there's a doctor here again."

"Interesting cases?"

"No, nothing interesting. Just the usual colds, symptoms of old age, and children with rickets. Your under-porter's wife's not at all well. Advanced myocarditis. But you know that already."

"Yes, I do," said the baron, and relapsed into deep thought.

"And what's wrong with you, baron?" I asked after a time. He started and looked at me.

"With me?" he exclaimed. "Nothing at all, I'm as fit as a fiddle, I'm never ill, I have an iron constitution."

Once more he fell silent and blew clouds of smoke into the air.

"An iron constitution," he repeated. "Listen, doctor, I know pretty well all the people in the village. One of the two men sitting in your waiting room, isn't his name Gause?"

"Yes, I think it is."

"He's a poor devil. I sometimes use him as a ploughman or a thresher. He's a poor devil, a kind of village philosopher. He thinks about the hereafter and divine justice and original sin and the immaculate conception and denies them all. Hasn't he yet told you that Christ wouldn't have died in AD 33 or 35 if the proletariat had been organised at that time?"

"No, he hasn't yet mentioned that to me. He comes here because of his rheumatism."

"His rheumatism? So he complains to you about his rheumatism? And what do you give him for it?"

"I give him aspirin and order him hot baths."

"That's perhaps the best thing," the baron said, and again relapsed into silence.

Suddenly he rose and began pacing up and down the room.

"I didn't think it was going to be so difficult," he said, glancing at me. "Really, I thought it was going to be much easier."

"Is there anything I can do for you, baron?" I asked.

He stopped.

"Yes, there is, doctor. There is something I would like you to do for me, and it's up to you to decide whether or not you can do it. It's only a small matter. Frankly, I don't know – well, the worst that can happen is that you'll say no."

He produced a small glass tube from his jacket pocket and uncorked it. It seemed to contain a few drops of watery fluid. He smelt it.

"The smell's horrible," he said with an embarrassed smile. "It's awful, it goes right up your nose. My assistant has not yet managed to make it odourless."

He handed me the tube.

"What is it?" I asked. "And what am I to do with it?"

"Gause's the man I need. If you could give him these drops in a glass of water or perhaps a cup of tea . . ."

"I don't quite understand. Is it a popular remedy for rheumatism or something?"

"Yes, that is – no, doctor, I don't want to lie to you. It has nothing to do with rheumatism. It's for an experiment I'm doing. A scientific experiment."

"But as a doctor I can't possibly use one of my patients as the object of your scientific experiments."

"Why not? We're both scientists, and so we're entitled to help one another. I guarantee that this drug can do no harm to the physical organism, and I take full responsibility for it. Its effects are purely mental, and they are only temporary. Perhaps it can make a person a little happier for a short time, that's all. So why shouldn't you help me?"

"Is it an opiate?" I asked.

"Something of the sort. If the experiment is successful, I'll tell you more about it, in fact I'll tell you everything about it. Look, I could offer the man a glass of schnapps. But there's that infernal smell and disgusting taste – he'd be suspicious at once. But medicine you gave him could have a nasty smell."

He turned and looked at the door.

59

"Are you sure they can't hear us outside?"

"Yes, quite sure. But I really don't know . . ."

"Whether you can trust me? It's true, you'd be putting yourself in my hands, but wouldn't I be putting myself in yours? I'm talking to the son of my dead friend. I'm working for an idea that was also his. He helped me with it. I realise I'm appealing to you in the name of a shade that is dear to you, but whatever is done in this matter is done for him and in his memory too. He would certainly have told you to do what I ask."

These words deprived me of all power of resistance.

"Very well, I'll do it," I said.

The baron took my hand and shook it.

"Thank you," he said. "You are doing me a great service, and I'm very grateful to you. It's quite simple and straightforward, isn't it? The whole contents – there are only three or four drops – in a cup of tea. There's also something else that I should like you to do, if you will. Tell the man – afterwards – that I want to talk to him. Tell him that I expect him tomorrow morning at ten o'clock sharp."

Then he left, without noticing how much I now regretted what I had agreed to do for him.

With the single exception of conscientiousness, perhaps, I lack pretty well all the qualities of a good doctor. Hardly had the baron shut the door behind him than my misgivings, doubts and self reproaches multiplied.

How had I been able to agree to such a proposition? How had the baron been able to put such an unreasonable proposition to me? I'm a doctor, I said to myself, am I to give a patient a drug about the nature, dosage and effects of which I know as good as nothing at all? Isn't that abusing the blind confidence the patient places in me? No, I can't keep the promise the baron extracted from me.

But then the voice of cowardice and convenience made itself heard. Was I really to go back on my word and disappoint the baron? He had assured me that the drug could not do the slightest harm to the physical organism, and he accepted sole responsibility for it, and finally he was a scientist and a researcher and was entitled to assume comprehension on my part.

Another voice inside me shouted no, no, no, and to put an end to my indecision and to avoid all future temptations I took the test tube and broke it and poured the contents on the floor. A pungent smell spread in the room and nearly made me sick.

I shouldn't have done that, I had no right to, I said to myself. I should have taken it back to the baron and said: Here it is, I can't keep my word, I can't do it. But I had no right to destroy it. What was I to do now? Go to the baron and tell him what I had done? No, I was too cowardly for that.

I found a way out. A pitiful, contemptible, deceitful, lying way out.

I pressed the juice of half a lemon into a glass of water. Then I added a few drops of tincture of iodine. The result smelt badly, and it might possibly produce a slight discomfort in the stomach, perhaps not even that. And the baron? He would assume his experiment had failed, and why should I worry about that?

I called the man whom the baron had talked about. He was a tall, thin fellow with a slight stoop. He had a stubbly chin and mistrustful eyes, and I now noticed for the first time that he really had the face of an introspective brooder. I had not looked at him properly before.

I pointed to the glass.

"That's for you," I said. "Drink it now. Come on, it's not so bad. Swallow it all. Well done. Here's aspirin to take at night, and remember, hot baths night and morning. And while I remember, the baron wants a word with you. He expects you at ten tomorrow morning, and don't be late."

He dropped his hat, picked it up, and put it on a chair. What I had said seemed to worry him. He drew his hand across his stubbly face.

"The baron?" he said. "Not the foreman?"

61

"No, the baron wants to talk to you himself."

He looked dismayed.

"The baron? Why should the baron want to talk to me?" he said. "The foreman sends for me sometimes in connection with work, but the baron? I've been here for five years and never yet . . . The neighbours must have . . . That little bit of wood? But everyone does it."

I tried to calm him down.

"No," I assured him, "it's certainly not about the wood."

He grew more agitated than ever.

"Oh? So it's not about wood I . . . ? Then I know what it is. He saw me sitting outside, and the way he looked at me . . . But how did he find out? Doctor, I swear to you that it only happened once, and I'll take an oath to that in court. On Christmas Eve there wasn't a bit of meat in the house, and my wife said . . ."

He didn't finish the sentence. With a violent movement he took his hat from the chair and stumbled out of the room.

That evening I went to see Bibiche.

I found her in front of her microscope. Her untouched supper was on the table, surrounded by crucibles, retorts and test tubes.

"It's so kind of you to think of me," she said. "I'm delighted you've come. Poor Bibiche! Work! I can't stop this evening."

She noticed my disappointment and smiled, but immediately grew serious again.

"I've changed greatly in the past year, haven't I?" she said. "I'm not the person I used to be. How am I to explain? I've become the vessel for an unusual and tremendous idea. It's not mine, I know, but it fills me completely and gives me no rest, I feel it in my veins, it mingles with all my thoughts, it has taken possession of me."

Once more she smiled.

"That sounds a little high-flown, perhaps. I'm only a minor technical assistant, but the work has gripped me – can you understand that? Don't look so gloomy, don't be angry with me. I'm so glad you came. Would you like to go for a walk with me tomorrow morning? An hour's walk before breakfast? Knock at my window at eight o'clock and I'll be ready. Definitely!"

I left. I walked a few yards from the house and stopped and gazed at the light in her window.

At nine o'clock the baron arrived. He did not see me. Bibiche herself opened the door. Then the shutters were closed.

I stood and waited for six hours in the snow and the cold. The baron did not emerge until three a.m.

I spent the rest of the night sleepless in my bed.

At eight a.m. I knocked at her window. Nothing stirred. I knocked again.

The front door opened and a small boy, he must have been about eleven years old, appeared with two empty milk cans under his arm.

He looked at me mistrustfully.

"The young lady's asleep," he said. "She's not to be disturbed."

To emphasise what he said he put his finger to his lips. Then he ran off and quickly disappeared.

For a short while I could still hear his two milk cans clinking in the mist.

ELEVEN

I believe that when I broke that test tube and emptied its contents on the carpet I missed a never to be repeated opportunity of decisively influencing the subsequent course of events. I have a vague and obscure feeling that perhaps everything would have turned out differently if I had done what Baron von Malchin asked. I did not, and it seemed to me that as a result I eliminated myself from everything that happened afterwards. I recognise in retrospect that I remained only a spectator – a spectator who was passionately involved in all I saw and heard but took no active part in it – and it is an irony of fate that I should be lying in this hospital bed, wounded, feverish and semi-paralysed, victim of the monstrous and inexplicable outcome.

I have no right to complain. I am alive. And I don't know what has happened to the others. Did the baron escape the hurricane of those last hours? And what happened to Federico? And she? Where did she take refuge? I have never doubted that she's alive and safe.

There is one person who could give me the answer. Praxatin keeps creeping into my room in that blue-and-white striped coat of his and with his broom, and he glances surreptitiously at me over his shoulder. I once said loudly to the nurse that I would enjoy a game of trente et quarante, but he behaved as if he were deaf. He is a coward, a terrible coward, and I hate him, just as I hated him that time when I unexpectedly met him at Bibiche's.

He greeted me, invited me to sit down, and made conversation. That was what I most resented. He behaved as if he were at home at Bibiche's, as if I were his guest and not hers. The priest, an old man with a bony face and white hair, was there too.

"You see in me a man who has had a busy day," he said while Bibiche handed me a cup of tea. "I think I can say that, because it's the truth. The baron has visitors, visitors from abroad, we often have foreign visitors. Do you realise what that means for me? It doesn't even leave me time to breathe. 'Arkady Fyodorovich,' the baron, my benefactor, said to me, 'please help by keeping your eye on the lunch and the dinner.' 'Of course,' I said, 'of course I'll keep my eye on things, I don't trust the kitchen staff, I'll make the fish salad myself.' But what happened? My little father the baron withdrew with his guests and conferred with them, and I didn't so much as catch sight of him all day long, he left everything to me. On such occasions I cannot help agreeing with my grandfather, who always said that work degraded men and turned them into animals. When I fetched that Sir Reginald from the station . . ."

"Arkady Fyodorovich," Bibiche interrupted, "you know that the baron doesn't like . . ."

"Yes, I know," said Praxatin. "When you frown, Kallisto, when you're displeased with me, it's as if the sun suddenly set in a clear sky. I know the gentlemen's wish to preserve their incognito, but there are certainly more than a dozen Sir Reginalds in England."

Once more he turned to me.

"Doctor," he said, "you look at me so searchingly with those scientist's eyes of yours that it's quite eerie. No doubt you're saying to yourself: low brow, prominent cheek bones, a weak person. That's what you think of me, isn't it? Vain and unreliable, thinks only of himself. Once upon a time I was such a person, perhaps, that is, a long time ago, when I was still carefree and still loved life. But now? Life has been hard for me, it has a rod for my back, and I became an entirely different person. Nowadays I nearly always think only of

65

others, I think of myself last of all. For instance, it now oppresses me more than I can say that you should now be sitting there so glumly, you haven't even drunk your tea. Kallisto, we must do something to entertain our guests. You must arrange a game for us."

Bibiche stroked my hand and whispered to me: "What's the matter? Are you upset?"

By now Praxatin had produced a pack of cards.

"Reverend sir," he said to the priest, "what about a game of trente et quarante, just for fun? You'll join us, won't you? I'll be banker."

"Are you just tired or has something upset you?" Bibiche asked in an undertone.

"You must excuse me, I don't play cards," the priest said. "I used sometimes to play a game of skat in the evening with my peasants at the White Hart, and occasionally I would play piquet with the baron. But now . . ."

"I play piquet too," the Russian said obligingly.

"To be frank with you," the priest explained, "my circumstances no longer permit me to expose myself to the risk of losing any money. Even when the game is for very low stakes. I have to count every penny."

This was true. I had already heard that he had to support his unemployed brother's huge family out of his stipend, though he supplemented this by letting nearly all the rooms of the priest's house to Bibiche and confining himself to the attic. A crucifix and a *Holy Family* on the wall in the room Bibiche used as a laboratory looked down on thermionic valves, litmus paper and Petri dishes filled with gelatine.

"If you lose, reverend sir, you can give me an IOU," the Russian suggested.

"That would be abusing your kindness," the priest said with a smile. "An IOU signed by me would probably be worth less than the paper it was written on. No, I really don't want to play."

The Russian put the cards back in his pocket.

"Then at least have a slice of this cake, reverend father," he said. "It's full of crushed elderberries and simmered blackberries. Doctor, you must try it too. You will honour me thereby. It's my own creation, the work of my own hands. For your information, doctor, we are today celebrating an important anniversary."

"That is so, we are celebrating it with a little improvised party," said the priest.

"Today," the Russian went on, "it is exactly a year since Kallisto arrived here to comfort us in our solitude. Kallisto, did I not give you my heart and my soul the first time I set eyes on you?"

"Indeed you did," said Bibiche, "and unless they have flown away in the meantime they must still be under a bell-jar in the lab."

There was something in what she said that put me to shame and drove the blood to my head. Had I not given her my heart and my soul the first time I set eyes on her? She knew that from that day on all my thoughts had circled round her, for I had confessed as much. Previously my attitude to her had been one of pride and reserve. And now? Effortlessly, with a look and just a few words, she had broken my pride. I was defenceless in relation to her, and she liked that. Sometimes she let me think I meant something to her, but that lasted only for a moment, and then she eluded me as skilfully as a pickpocket. Why did I see through all this only now? It was me, not Prince Praxatin, whom she was mocking.

A wave of grief and bitterness rose inside me, and I stood up.

"So it's an intimate little party," I said. "I don't want to be in the way any longer."

She looked at me in surprise.

"You want to go?" she said. "Why? Do stay. You can't? Why not? You can't stay even if I ask you?"

I did not stay, but said goodbye. I noted with bitter satisfaction that Bibiche made no further effort to detain me.

Back in my lodgings I flung myself on the sofa. Once more everything seemed to have changed. I was upset, at a loss what to do, furious with myself. I recalled every word Bibiche had said, tormenting myself over and over again. My head ached, perhaps I was feverish. "Even if I ask you to stay?" she had said, and in spite of that I had gone, I had behaved badly and offended her. "Are you upset?" she had said. Now she must be tired of my sulks. If only I could make amends. Supposing I went back? Now, straight away, with some flowers? I'd say I just wanted to bring you these roses, Bibiche, because today it's just a year since you came here, that's the only reason I went. But where was I to get roses here, in winter? There are some hideous, dusty artificial flowers in the vase over there, I said to myself, why hasn't the baron got a greenhouse? If he had a greenhouse instead of a laboratory – but then Bibiche wouldn't be here. Elderberries, I saw white elderberries somewhere today, where was that? No, crushed elderberries, his "creation". If I brought her my heart and soul, perhaps she'd put them under a bell-jar and laugh . . .

There was a knock at the door, and I started. The small boy who had taken two milk cans from the priest's house came in. He looked round the room and spotted me lying on the sofa.

"Good evening, this is from the young lady," he said, and handed me a folded note.

I sprang to my feet and read it. It said: "You're angry with me and I don't know why. Poor Bibiche! I must talk to you before the day's over. I'm dining at the baron's, meet me at eleven o'clock outside the park gate. Definitely. I can't come earlier."

She had crossed out "definitely" and written "please" instead.

The north wind blew frozen snow in my face in the village street. I froze, and waited, waited for a quarter of an hour. Eleven o'clock struck. I heard noises from the park, footsteps crunched in the snow, the gate opened. "Who's there?" someone called out, and a cone of light from a pocket torch shone first on my feet and then on my body and head.

68

"Is that you, doctor? You go for walks at night at this time of year?" the baron said.

Bibiche appeared out of the dark beside him – an unhappy and upset Bibiche.

She looked at me helplessly, like a child expecting to be slapped. I couldn't help it, he insisted on coming with me, I read in her eyes.

"Come along, doctor, we'll take the child home," said the baron. I wasn't angry with her for a moment, on the contrary, I was delighted to see her and find that between us everything was as it had been before. She noticed this at once and put her arm in mine.

"You can be utterly intolerable," she remarked with conviction.

On the way to the priest's house the baron was as talkative as usual.

'I still have to thank you for making my little experiment possible, doctor," he said.

This gave me an uncomfortable feeling. Though I had not kept my word he thanked me – worse still, I had deceived him. Perhaps I should have told him the truth, but I thought it wiser to tell him nothing.

"Did the man come and see you?" I asked.

"Yes, and he quoted the Bible at me, the Book of Job, the psalms and the Epistle to the Corinthians, and he accused himself of having stolen wood from the forest, and he confessed that he shot a roe-deer on Christmas Eve."

"Are you going to charge him?"

"What do you take me for, doctor? I'm not a monster. He came and confessed, it was more or less what I expected. I was not certain that the experiment would succeed with an individual. It did."

We had reached the priest's house. Bibiche was leaning against the door, struggling to keep awake.

"Are you tired?" the baron asked.

"Very," she said. "I've been walking in my sleep. I'm not as used to strong wine as the younger of your two guests."

The baron smiled. "It's quite all right to say whom you met this evening. One of my two guests is a former governor of a British crown colony. He's retired now, and he's the leader of the legitimist movement in England. My other guest? The young lady standing here, holding her hand over her mouth to prevent us from seeing that she's yawning, has discreetly refrained from telling you that she dined with the King of England."

"The King of England?" I exclaimed in amazement, looking at Bibiche.

"Yes, with Richard XI," she said. "I'm falling over with tiredness. Good night."

"But the King of England isn't called Richard XI," I pointed out.

"Richard XI of the House of Tudor," the baron explained. "At present an art teacher at a girls' school in Sussex. To English legitimists he is the rightful king."

TWELVE

It cannot have been by chance that on my way back from the forester's lodge I met Baron von Malchin at the edge of the pine wood. It was early morning, he had been shooting, his bag was two black grouse and a goshawk, and even then I had the definite impression that he had not strayed far from the place where the path emerges from the wood and had been waiting for me. I now know what was in his mind. The closer he was to the end of his experiments, the greater became his need to talk about them. There is a mental equilibrium that is imperilled if one condemns oneself to silence. The baron needed to talk.

For a year he had confided his secret to his technical assistant Bibiche, and no doubt he had earlier confided a great deal to the priest who, however, had ended by disappointing him. The old man had put up a quiet resistance to his idea that he had been unable to overcome. He wanted someone before whose eyes he could re-erect the mighty edifice of his ambitious plans. From the outset he had put his trust in me, the son of his old friend.

I emerged from the wood under a clear, pale blue sky. The ice needles hanging from the branches of the pine trees shimmered in the pale sunlight. The distant barking of dogs came from the village, whose square bell-tower was still out of sight.

The baron saw me and came towards me across the marshy fields with his gun in his hand.

"Good morning, doctor," he said, "don't go that way, if

you do you'll soon be up to your knees in snow, come with me, I'll show you a better way."

He started by talking about his guests, who had left the day before – I had caught a fleeting glimpse of them – and then about shooting. For a time he talked about nothing but short-haired terriers and stalking, roe-deer and red grouse. I don't remember how he made the transition to politics.

He declared himself to be a monarchist and a legitimist. He defined legitimism as belief in submission to a higher will. Providence worked more effectively through the hereditary principle than through the popular will – if there was such a thing as the latter which, in his opinion, remained to be proved. Monarchism, he maintained, needed no sociological justification in our age or any other. It was not tied to any age, it was not a superior kind of state organisation but simply the only kind for which there was justification. Belief in it was an integral part of his religion.

These were arguable propositions and did not particularly surprise me when put forward by a country nobleman. But then he went on to say casually, as if it were an obvious proposition with which I had been long familiar: "If Germany, if Europe is to have a future, it must be associated with the revival of the Holy Roman Empire."

"What are you suggesting?" I exclaimed in surprise. "You dream about the revival of the Holy Roman Empire? Wasn't that a world-wide joke for centuries?"

He admitted that this was the case.

"Yes, it was a joke for centuries, or rather that's what it was under the House of Habsburg, under whom it lost its meaning, its substance and its strength. It can be revived only under a dynasty summoned by providence and sanctified by history."

"So you believe that if the Hohenzollerns came back . . ."

"The Hohenzollerns?" he interrupted me. "What an idea, doctor. The Margraves of Brandenburg and Kings of Prussia were strangers in their own country. The Empire of the Hohenzollerns is a closed chapter in the history of Germany. The

72

Hohenzollerns? My relations with the last wearer of the imperial crown were purely personal."

He stopped and listened to the hoarse cry of a nutcracker that came from a long way away in the wood. Then he went on, quietly, as if he were talking to himself and not to me: "The old Empire of dream and legend – have you forgotten that under the Hohenstaufen it was the heart of the world? The Hohenstaufen were not kings by grace of the princes."

"No," I said as we walked on. "But the Hohenstaufen are dead. Their dynasty, the only really imperial dynasty that the world has seen since the days of Augustus, is extinct."

"No, it is not," the baron said after a brief silence. "It still lives, and in accordance with its destiny it will one day assume the crown and the mantle, even if in the meantime those sacred insignia have been sold off to the Americans."

I looked at him. The passionate, fanatical expression that I already knew had returned to his face. Quarrelling with him now might be dangerous. Nevertheless I said: "I ask you, baron, where your thoughts are straying. There may still be a Tudor lurking obscurely somewhere in England. But the Hohenstaufen dynasty perished more than six hundred years ago in a sea of blood and tears. 'Let the heavens rejoice, let the earth be jubilant that the name and the body, the seed and the offspring of the King of Babylon have been exterminated,' the Pope declared. The King of Babylon was Frederick II, the son of Henry and Constance, the last Hohenstaufen to wear the imperial crown."

"Frederick II, who was called *stupor mundi*, the wonder of the world and its wonderful transformer," the baron said. "For his sake Constance left her beloved convent, too, after she learnt in a dream that she would bear 'the firebrand, the light of the world, the mirror without flaw'. The princes of the whole world bowed to him, and when he died the sun went down, according to the chronicler, and the people took him away to Kyffhäuser. He had five sons."

"Yes, five sons. Henry, the son of Isabella of England, died

73

aged fifteen. The other Henry, son of the Princess of Aragon, died by his own hand."

"The Henry who betrayed the Empire, the dark-haired boy, who sang in the morning and wept in the evening in his prison. He jumped into the sea from the prison walls."

"The third son," I went on, "Conrad, the King of Rome, died of the plague when he was twenty-six."

The baron shook his head.

"He died of poison and not of the plague," he said, "and in his last hours he foresaw the future. 'The Empire is fading away and will sink into the oblivion of death,' he said. What a prophecy."

We crossed a field of stubble, and the solidly frozen grass stems tinkled like glass beneath our feet. A big bird rose steeply right in front of us and disappeared with broad wing-beats over the snow-covered wood.

I broke the silence.

"The Emperor's fourth son was Manfred, who was killed in the Battle of Benevento."

"Manfred, who forgot his kingdom because of his songs," said the baron. "All the Hohenstaufen sang. His body was found days later among the many dead on the battlefield, he was recognised by his fair hair and his skin, which was as white as snow. *Biondo e bello e di gentile aspetto* was how Dante described him, and in the *Purgatory* pictured him smiling and showing his wounds and complaining of the Pope's thirst for vengeance and refusal to let him be buried under the bridge at Benevento. Manfred had two sons who were as fair as he. They died after lying in chains for thirty years in Charles of Anjou's prisons."

"And Enzio, the Emperor's favourite son," I went on, "died imprisoned by the Bolognesi. The Emperor offered them 'a ring of silver round the city' as ransom for him and reminded them of the fickleness of fortune, which raised men up on high only to end by sending them crashing down to destruction. But the Bolognesi refused to release the Emperor's son. 'We hold him and we shall keep him,' they replied, 'and a small dog has often caught a wild boar.' Enzio lived two years afer the death of the young Conradin, his nephew, who was executed in the market square at Naples. He was the last of the Hohenstaufen."

"No," said the baron, "he was not the last of that noble line. Handsome and attractive as he was even in his decline, he found himself a mistress in prison. The youngest daughter of the Ghibelline Count Niccolo Ruffo secretly shared her bed with him. They were married on a carnival night while his guards were carousing in the streets. He died three days later, and she left the city. Their child was born at Bergamo."

Suddenly we were standing at the park gate. I could see the protective covering of straw round the stems of the roses, the well, the terrace and steep blue roof of the manor house. I was surprised, because I could not remember how we had got to the village.

We had to wait. Two ox-carts laden with dung had got entangled with each other and blocked the way. The wheels creaked, the oxen bellowed, the drivers swore, and in spite of the din Baron von Malchin went on talking.

"The Pope knew of Enzio's son," he said. "'Out of mercy and Christian love let us not remember him,' Clement IV said. The Hohenstaufen survived in Bergamo through the centuries in poverty and obscurity. They passed on the secret of their heritage from generation to generation, as well as the two books in which King Enzio wrote his songs and romances. The man I sought out in Bergamo eleven years ago still possessed them. He made his living as a carpenter and, as he was poor, he entrusted me with his son and I took him with me."

Baron von Malchin pointed over the two interlocked dung carts to the reddish sandstone walls up which bare shoots of wild vine climbed.

"You see the house? That is the Kyffhäuser where the secret Emperor lives and waits. I am preparing the way for him, and one day I shall repeat to the world the words that Manfred's Saracen servant called out to the citizens of the rebellious city of Viterbo: 'Open your gates, open your hearts, for your lord and master, the Emperor's son, has come.'"

The baron fell silent and looked at the two ox-carts which had at last disengaged themselves and were advancing creakingly down the village street. Then, without looking at me and with a timid and embarrassed smile he added in a completely changed voice: "You'll find him over there in the garden pavilion, where he works. At this time of day he's generally having a French lesson."

THIRTEEN

I have thought a great deal about what must have happened inside me after Baron von Malchin revealed his extraordinary plans to me in the village street. After he left me I seem at first to have been completely under the spell of what he said. Behind it I felt the force of an unusually strong will, and I must already have felt obscurely that it was backed by real forces or abilities that were unknown to me. Not for one moment did I feel that he was a phantast, on the contrary, I had a presentiment that he represented a danger to me and to the world in which I had hitherto lived. These misgivings were then partially suppressed by doubts and resistances that rose inside me, and for a time my mind was the battleground of weird, absurd and conflicting ideas – and I felt distinctly that I was feverish.

What I did next was an attempt to escape from these ideas. While absent-mindedly and ditheringly looking for my thermometer – I was shivering with cold though there was a fire in the grate – I suddenly remembered what the schoolmaster had said to me on the day after my arrival at Morwede. "You're too trusting," he had said. "If you want to know the truth about anyone here in the village, ask me."

After that I couldn't stand it in my room for another moment, but went to find him. I asked where he lived, and a little girl pointed out his house to me.

He met me on the steps in cycling cape and green felt hat. "Ah, doctor, there you are, delighted to see you," he said unnecessarily loudly. "Come in, come in. I've been expecting you for two days. You're not detaining me, not in the least.

It's Sunday, and I can do what I like with my time. Dagobert, we have a visitor. I knew you would be coming, doctor."

He took my hand and led me into a room which smelt of methylated spirits and wet loden cloth. A herbarium lay open on the table among all sorts of algae, lichens and mosses. I noticed a cast iron boot-hook shaped like a stag beetle protruding from under the sofa. Spirit glasses containing the edible and poisonous mushrooms of the neighbourhood were arranged in two rows on the chest-of-drawers. A young hedgehog was drinking milk from a stone dish on the floor.

"That's Dagobert," the schoolmaster explained. "My only friend since the departure of your unforgettable predecessor. A prickly little friend, but you only have to know him. He and I are alike, aren't we?"

He cleared an armchair for me on which a dibble, a pair of tweezers, some sausage wrapped in newspaper and a clothes brush were lying, and made me sit down.

"Things have been happening, haven't they?" he began. "Presumably the distinguished visitors whose presence has been honouring the village have given you food for thought, haven't they? I thought as much. Was a confidential emissary of the Quai d'Orsay on a semi-official mission among them by any chance? Did he come here to meet a scion of the Jagiellons who argued his claim to the Polish throne? Or was it a fat and not very clean Levantine who claims to be a direct descendant of the imperial house of Byzantium? Yes, my dear sir, such people exist, why shouldn't they? Four months ago there was a man here who didn't look very imperial, it's true, he looked more like an oriental money-changer. Was there another one this time? Not Alexius VII? Well, this time it could have been the real Alexius, there were several imperial houses in Byzantium, the Comneni, the Angeli . . ."

"Tell me, for heaven's sake, what's the meaning of all this?" I interrupted him.

He was holding a moss under his magnifying glass and using a small knife and a needle to free the spores.

"I admit that it all must be rather confusing to you," he said without looking up from what he was doing. "But if you consider what goes on behind the scenes . . . Assuming, for instance, that a certain person formerly lived a very adventurous life, and perhaps – I lay emphasis on perhaps – had peculiar tendencies and came into contact with all sorts of people, and these people now turn up one after another and demand money to keep silent. Many of them look as if they might be gentlemen – they are generally secret emissaries, statesmen, politicians – but there are also questionable types with whom one should not really allow oneself to be seen – they allow rumours to be spread that they are the descendants of emperors and kings and are now living in reduced circumstances. When such people are around there are important consultations and secret conferences – at all events that sounds much better and more impressive than admitting that one has fallen into the hands of gentry of doubtful reputation who leave with money by the cartload."

"Is this all true that you're telling me?" I asked in dismay.

The schoolmaster looked at me over his spectacles.

"No," he said, "it's nothing but fairy tales for credulous people, and you're not one of them. So you don't really have to believe a word I say. Nor do you have to believe that every year the baron has to sell off a parcel of woodland or agricultural land. It's all nothing but a product of the imagination, my dear sir, a high spirited joke. And if a descendant of Alaric the King of the Goths turns up next week – my Dagobert comes of ancient lineage too, his ancestors lived with us in the Tertiary period, but he doesn't threaten me or ask anything of me – all he wants from me is a little milk and a little kindness, isn't that so, Dagobert?"

For a short while he watched the hedgehog, which had emptied the bowl of milk and was nibbling at a bit of sausage skin on the floor. Then he went on: "Yes, and there's also that Federico you'll have been wondering about. That's a different kettle of fish altogether. You will aready have guessed that he's the baron's illegitimate son – everyone in the village knows it,

79

though there are differences of opinion about the boy's mother. There are those who claim he's the son of a dead sister of the baron. I don't share that opinion. But the boy presents him with problems. He attained sexual maturity at an early age and is in love with the little girl Elsie. Now do you understand why the baron had to move her out of the house? Incest. Where could the boy have got that from? Yes, our friend the baron has his problems."

He went on, without giving me time to ask any questions: "And then there's that so-called technical assistant of his. Now, *there*'s a joke for you. The laboratory is of course merely a pretext. The fact that the baron puts her up at the priest's house adds a special piquancy to the situation. Very clever I must say, perhaps a little too clever. Whom did he fetch her from Berlin for? Only for himself, or also for his special friend, that Russian prince – nobody knows what he's really there for. I offer no opinion on the matter. Perhaps they're in collusion, there are types who begrudge each other nothing. Another possibility is that the baron is the duped party. It's a fact that the priest keeps both eyes shut about the goings on in his house."

I don't know what else the schoolmaster went on to tell me. At this point my memory becomes very confused. I can only assume that I kept my composure sufficiently to prevent him from noticing what was going on inside me. I dimly remember having to look through a thick notebook, I have no idea what was in it, he may have wanted me to read his poems. I also remember looking at a book with illustrations of lichens and mosses. Then we seem to have left the house together and gone for a long walk. I remember the flourish with which he raised his felt hat when he met someone on the main road, and how he turned and hurried back towards the village as if he had suddenly become afraid of me.

I must then have wandered about alone for some time. That evening I found stones in my pocket, and I have no idea why I picked them up. Perhaps it was to frighten away a dog that followed me along the road. I left my hat and coat lying somewhere near the fish pond, where it was found next day by the innkeeper's daughter who was going to the station in her wicker buggy.

There is no trace in my memory of how I got back to the village in my thin jacket. I can remember nothing at all of what happened until the moment when I was standing in the laboratory.

Bibiche's voice came through the open door from the next room.

"You can come in in a moment. Don't turn round. What's the time, and why don't you knock if you want to come in?'

FOURTEEN

She came towards me in a yellow Chinese silk kimono and red silk slippers and with a smile that seemed to say: Do you like me in this? She smiled at me, and the smile froze in her lovely, open face, and gave way to an expression of alarm.

"Where have you been?" she asked. "Why are you looking at me like that? What's the matter?"

"Nothing," I said. I had difficulty in finding the words, and my voice sounded strange to me. "I've been for a walk, and I've come to ask you something."

She looked at me inquiringly.

"Well? Ask, then. What do you look like? But sit down."

She put a cushion on the floor and another on top of it, and squatted with her arms round her knees and her face towards me.

"Why don't you sit down?" she said. "Good. And now talk. I'm free for exactly half an hour."

"Exactly half an hour," I repeated after her. "And then? Who's coming then? The baron or the Russian prince?"

"The baron," she replied. "But does it matter?"

"No, it doesn't, it's all the same to me, everything's all the same to me now I know . . ."

She raised her head slightly.

"You know what?" she asked.

Her calmness put me out.

"I know enough," I managed to stammer out. "I know quite enough. He comes in the afternoon, and he comes in the evening, and he stays till three o'clock in the morning . . ."

"Quite right," she said. "You're well informed. I go to bed much too late, and I need a lot of sleep. Poor Bibiche . . . Is that all? So you're jealous of the baron. I admit that gives me pleasure: it shows you care for me a little. You have never said so, though we have known each other such a long time. On the other hand, you have sometimes been really nasty to me, but that has been forgiven, Bibiche is magnanimous. So you love me . . ."

"No longer," I said, infuriated by her sarcastic tone.

"Really?" she said. "Is it all over? What a pity. Do you always get over it so quickly?"

"Bibiche," I exclaimed in desperation. "Why do you torment me like this? You're making fun of me. Just tell me the truth and I'll go."

"The truth?" she said, now quite serious again. "I really don't know what you're talking about. I've always been absolutely frank and honest with you – perhaps too frank and honest. A woman should never be that."

I jumped to my feet.

"Are things to go on like this? I can't stand it any longer. Do you think I don't know that the whole thing, the work and all that" – I pointed to the open door of the laboratory – "is a sham, and that he tells people you're his technical assistant though in reality . . ."

"Well? Say it. That in reality I'm his mistress. Isn't that what you were going to say?"

"Yes, or Prince Praxatin's."

She raised her head and looked at me, taken aback, and with big, frightened eyes. Then she retreated into herself.

"Praxatin's mistress," she muttered. "Almighty God."

She rose and flung the cushions on the sofa.

"Mistress of that lout, that bear. And the whole thing, the work, the laboratory, Our Lady's Fire, the whole thing just a pretext . . . Tell me just one thing, what gave you that idea . . . ? No, tell me nothing, I don't want an answer, tell me nothing at all, please, I don't want to hear it. All I want to

83

know is how you plucked up courage to say that to me, because it needed courage, and what gave you the right . . ."

"Please forgive me," I said. "I really had no right to walk in here, to take your time and to trouble you with reproaches. That is now clear to me. If you will be kind enough to accept my apologies, I will go."

"Yes," she said. "I think that perhaps it will be better if you go."

I bowed.

"I shall ask the baron to accept my resignation today."

I turned to go. Grief and despair had me by the throat. When I reached the door she quietly said: "Stay."

I took no notice.

She stamped her foot. "I said: Stay."

I was in the laboratory. I stopped, but only for a moment, and then walked on without looking round. But then she was by my side.

"Can't you hear me? Don't go. Do you think I could stand life here without you?"

She seized my wrists.

"Listen," she said. "Whatever happened in my life, I have loved only one man, and he didn't know it, or didn't want to know it, and he doesn't believe me now. I've just been to Berlin, and do you know what was the first thing I did? I went to the institute and asked after you. Look me in the face. Do I look like a liar? I can't even pretend."

She dropped my hands.

"You were quite pale when you came in, deathly pale – why didn't I tell you all this straight away? You still don't believe me? You soon will. I'm coming to see you – do you understand what I'm saying? Perhaps it would have been better if you had left me time. But I don't want you to go on tormenting yourself with such thoughts. I'll be with you the day after tomorrow – do you believe me at last? At nine o'clock, when the whole village is asleep. All you have to do is to make sure the front door isn't bolted. Well, then, go. No, stay."

She flung her arms round me and kissed me, and I held her in my arms.

Something crashed to the floor. I felt I was rising out of an abyss, rising more and more quickly and eventually at lightning speed, not standing but lying outstretched, and then I heard a voice, a man's voice, saying: "Too stupid, how can one be so clumsy?"

We let each other go.

"Who's there?" I called out in alarm.

Bibiche laughed and looked at me in surprise.

"What's the matter with you, there's nobody here, how could anyone be here, do you imagine I let myself be kissed in public? You're here and I'm here, isn't that enough?"

"But somebody spoke quite loud. I heard him."

"It was you," she said, "don't you know that? 'How can one be so clumsy,' you said, you said it yourself, and you don't know it. Your nerves must be in a bad way. Look what we've done."

She pointed to a heap of shattered glass on the floor.

"No great disaster," she said. "It's only a bowl with an artificial culture medium with agar agar. But one shouldn't kiss in a laboratory, please note. If we'd upset the cultures over there – it doesn't bear thinking about, no, leave the broken glass, I'll clear it up."

"Bibiche," I said. "Where's the Our Lady's Fire?"

She looked at me in surprise.

"What do you know about that?"

"Nothing," I answered. "I heard you mention it and I can't get it out of my head. You were talking about your work and Our Lady's Fire."

She suddenly seemed to be in a hurry to get me out of the laboratory.

"Oh. Did I? I don't know whether I should talk about it. Besides, it's late. You must go, darling. Haven't you got a hat? Where's your overcoat? No overcoat in this weather? That's foolhardy. You obviously need someone to look after you."

When it began to get dark that evening I stood at the window of my consulting room and looked down at the village street.

Snow was falling. It was thin, light and noiseless as it floated down. Things lost their shape, grew ghostly and strange.

A flock of crows rose squawking from a rowan tree, and soon afterwards a hunting sleigh came down the street at speed. The driver was Federico. I recognised him only when he half rose and greeted me as he passed.

When he had gone I had in my mind's eye, not his boyish face, but the Gothic relief in the antique dealer's shop at Osnabrück that still haunted me. I don't know how it happened, but I suddenly remembered what I had been searching for in my mind for so long, that is, where I had first seen that marble head and its remote smile. The memory came back to me with the force of a vivid experience. The head was part of a bad copy of the tremendous relief in the cathedral of Palermo that shows the last Hohenstaufen emperor as Caesar and conquering hero.

With that the web of lies that the schoolteacher had so skilfully spun collapsed as lightly and noiselessly as the snow descending from the roofs. I sighed with relief at liberation from the nightmare. All he had said about Bibiche, the baron and Federico's origin was false. For Federico bore in his boyish face the terrible and noble features of Frederick II, the Wonder of the World and its marvellous transformer.

The sun went down behind heavy, dark clouds that glowed violent and scarlet, sulphur green and copper yellow, looking as if they were on fire. Never before had I seen such colours in the sky. And a strange idea came to me. It seemed to me that that gleaming and glowing, that fiery blazing up and dying down in the evening sky, was a game of Bibiche's called Our Lady's Fire, and that it came, not from the setting sun, but from here below, from her, from the small, ill-lit room in which she had kissed me.

FIFTEEN

I found out what the baron meant by his life's work from a conversation that began with some exchanges between him and the priest and a remark of Bibiche's. We were sitting in the manor house hall, which was furnished in farmhouse style. I still have a clear picture of it in my mind: the oak chests, the brightly painted chairs round the massive table, the wood carving of *Ecce Homo* on the staircase wall and the big 'lolling bench' by the fireplace that nowadays is seldom to be found in Westphalian farmhouse rooms. The priest had a glass of wine in front of him, and the rest of us were drinking whisky. Bibiche was resting her head on the back of her left hand and drawing geometrical figures on a sheet of paper, spirals, small circles and rosettes. Prince Praxatin was sitting slightly apart and playing patience.

I do not know how the conversation began. I was sunk in my own thoughts and had not been listening. When she looked up from her doodling Bibiche, sitting opposite me, acted as if we were strangers. Did she remember the promise she had given me the day before, or had that been the result of a fleeting, momentary mood? I wanted certainty in the matter, and asked her across the table whether she was going to be in the laboratory at nine o'clock next day. She shrugged her shoulders without looking up and then, instead of circles and spirals, drew an elaborate and highly ornamental figure nine on the sheet of paper.

"What you point out," I heard the baron saying, "applies to any age, not only to ours. The great symbols – the crown, the sceptre, Mithras and the apple – are created and maintained by faith. Humanity has forgotten how to believe in those symbols. Anyone able to rekindle the glow of faith in an age that has grown tepid and empty will find it easy to lead the hearts of mankind back to the glamour of the throne and the idea of empire by the grace of God."

"Faith is a blessing," said the priest. "It is a result of God working in us, and it can be kindled only by patient work, by loving service, and by prayer."

"No," said Bibiche, speaking as out of a dream. "It can also be kindled by chemistry."

There was silence in the room, you could have heard a pin drop. I looked in surprise at Bibiche, who was once more bent over her doodling, and then at the priest. His face was unmoved, but on his lips there was a trace of displeasure and weary dissent.

"What do you mean by what you have just said?" I asked Bibiche. "What are we to understand by it?"

The baron answered for her.

"What we mean by it?" he said. "You as a doctor know that all our feelings – fear, love, sadness, happiness, despair – all our physiological signs of life, are the result of quite definite chemical processes in our body. From recognition of that fact to what my colleague succinctly said is only a small step."

Bibiche had gone, leaving the paper on which she had been drawing on the table. The priest and Praxatin had also gone without my noticing it, and the strange thing was that I was not in the least surprised at their disappearance. Not for a moment did I wonder why I had been left alone with the baron.

"Only a small step," Baron von Malchin went on. "But how much work was needed before I could take it. How many sleepless nights did I have to spend, how much reading and study did I have to do, how many doubts did I have to overcome. The starting-point was something your father said. 'What we call the fervour and ecstasy of faith,' he said to me in this room, sitting at this table, 'whether as an individual

88

phenomenon or as a group phenomenon, nearly always presents the clinical picture of a state of excitation produced by a hallucinogenic drug. But what hallucinogenic drug produces this effect? None is known to science.'"

"I can't believe that my father said that," I protested. "There is no hint of any such idea in anything he wrote. The statement you have attributed to him is blasphemy."

"Blasphemy? That is a hard word," the baron replied with equanimity. "Is it appropriate or relevant when the sole objective is discovery and establishment of the truth? Is it blasphemy if I say that a feeling as noble as contempt for death can be produced by a small dose of heroin, or a feeling of greater happiness by opium or the ecstasy of lust by cantharidin? In tropical Central America there is said to be a plant which, if chewed for several days or hours, bestows the gift of prophecy – did you know that? If we follow the history of faith through the ages . . ."

"So what you are saying," I interrupted, "is that the tremendous spiritual upheaval that turned the man of the world Inigo de Recalde into St Ignatius of Loyola was the result of a hallucinogenic drug?"

"Let us leave that aside," the baron said. "That way won't get us any further. My starting-point was that there must be drugs capable of producing religious ecstasy, both individually and collectively. No such drugs are known to science, and it was recognition of that fact that set me off on my task."

He leant over the table and swept the ashes of his half-smoked cigar into the ashtray in front of me.

"Blasphemy, you said," he went on. "I followed the path that my research showed me. At first I had great difficulties. I worked for a year without the slightest success."

He rose. We were still in the hall, but immediately afterwards we must have left the house, because what he went on to say is associated in my mind with a different background. In my mind's eye I see the baron and me stopping in the village street near my lodgings, the air was clear and frosty, and I remember

89

distinctly that while he was quoting the neo-Platonist Dionysus two petrol cans and a crate of beer were unloaded outside the shop door and a man with a dogwood stick and a peaked cap emerged from the inn and greeted us as he passed. I must then have gone for a walk with the baron, for we reached open country and came across two men roasting potatoes on a very smoky fire of brushwood. Enumeration of the various names of the parasites of wheat is associated in my mind with the odour of resin and charred wood and of roasting potatoes. Then we were back in the manor house, sitting in the baron's study with all those ancient weapons hanging on the walls. But the baron must have been in a restless state, for he ended his tale where he had begun it, in the hall, where the others, the priest and Bibiche were too, and Prince Praxatin was sitting at the head of the table playing patience – they seemed to have been there all the time, and everything was as it had been before, except that now it was getting dark and Bibiche rose and lit the lamps.

SIXTEEN

"Yes, for a year I made no progress," the baron said. "I was on the wrong track. The time I spent on the scientific works of Greek and Latin authors was wasted. The few clues I found or thought I found in the *Plant Book* of Zenobius of Agrigentum, the *Description of Cultivated Plants* by Theophrastus of Eresos, in Dioscorides's *Materia Medica* and in Claudius Piso's *Book of Medicines* turned out to be misleading, or told me things that were common knowledge. A misinterpretation of a passage in one of these authors made me believe for a long time that I had found the characteristics I wanted in henbane, *Hyoscyamus niger*, and later in white dead-nettle. I was mistaken in both cases. You already know that the poison in henbane produces nothing but motor excitation, and the sap of the dead-nettle can sometimes cause slight inflammation of the skin, but nothing else."

The baron picked up the bottle of whisky and a glass, but he was so carried away by his ideas that he poured the whisky on to the table-top and the floor. He went on talking without noticing this and with the empty bottle still in his hand.

"When I turned from the scientific to the religious and philosophical writings of antiquity, I found the first references that pointed to the correctness of my theory. Diodorus Siculus, a contemporary of Julius Caesar and Augustus, mentions in one of his works a plant which 'removes him who tastes it from ordinary existence and elevates him to the gods.' He does not mention the plant's name and gives no further description of it. Nevertheless this passage was of great importance to me.

This was the first clear and unequivocal reference that connects the state of religious ecstasy with the consumption of a poisonous plant. My theory had passed the stage of mere conjecture. It was supported by the testimony of an author whose conscientiousness caused him to be used often and without hesitation as a historical source by historians of the later imperial period."

The baron stopped and returned the greeting of two men who were driving a snow plough down the street, and he had a short conversation with one of them about a sick cow. "It won't do," he called out after the man, "if she won't touch clover fodder, she has fever." As soon as the snow plough had gone he went on with his story:

"A few months later I came across the incomparably more important testimony of Dionysus the Areopagite, a fourth-century Christian neo-Platonist, who states in one of his works that he imposed a two-day fast on the members of his community, who longed for the real presence of God, and he then regaled them with 'bread made with holy flour'. 'For this bread,' he writes, 'leads to union with God and enables us to understand the infinite' – are you getting tired, doctor? Really not? After finding this passage I felt compensated for all the work I had done previously. Bread made of 'holy flour'. I recalled a passage in the Bible that I had not taken account of previously because I had failed to appreciate its real significance. 'He called corn out of the earth so that men might eat of it and recognise Him,' it says in the Book of Kings. And in the sacred writings of the Parsees there are continual references to the 'ears of corn of purification', and in an ancient Roman mystery play there is reference to a white or pale kind of corn by which 'the good goddess makes human beings see', in other words, a crop that has disappeared, displaced perhaps by other cultivated plants – what forgotten kind of wheat has white ears?"

He paused.

"But all this was following a false scent. I was going up a blind alley that led nowhere," he went on, "and heaven knows where it might have led me but for the fact that I came across an ancient

Roman rural priests' song, a solemn invocation of Marmar or Mavor, who at that time was not yet the bloodthirsty god of war but the peaceful protector of the fields. 'Let your white frost invade the crop so that they acknowledge thy power,' it said. Like all priests, Roman rural priests knew the secret of the hallucinogenic drug that produces a state of ecstasy in which people 'become seeing' and 'acknowledge the power of the god'. The white frost was not a kind of wheat, but a wheat disease, a parasite, a fungus that invaded the wheat and fed on its substance."

The baron's eye wandered across the fields and meadows that lay silent under their covering of snow. A tiny field mouse scurried past us, leaving an almost invisible trail behind.

"There are many kinds of parasitic fungi," the baron went on, "the ascomycetes, the phycomycetes, and the basidiomycetes. In his *Synopsis Fungorum* Bargin describes more than a hundred varieties, and nowadays his work is regarded as out-of-date. But among that hundred I had identified the only one that produces ecstatic effects when it is introduced into human food and thus finds its way into the human organism."

He bent down and picked up a potato that was lying in the snow near the fire. He looked at it attentively, and then put it back where it had come from as carefully as if it were a treasure. The two men who had approached inquisitively looked at him in surprise, and one of them threw brushwood on the fire.

"Yes," said the baron, "it was the only one among a hundred different varieties. The only information I had about the clinical picture of the disease was that the fungus caused discoloration of the bracts. I seemed to be confronted with a pretty hopeless task, but a simple observation came to my aid. There is – or was – a wheat disease that was often described in earlier centuries and was known by a different name wherever it appeared. In Spain it was called Mary Magdalene's Plait, in Alsace it was known as Poor Soul's Dew. In Adam of Cremona's *Physician's Book* it was called Misericord Seed, and in the Alps it was called St Peter's Snow. In the St Gallen area it was known as the Mendicant Friar, and in northern Bohemia as St John's Rot. Here in Westphalia, where it appeared especially often, the peasants called it Our Lady's Fire."

"Oh," I said, "so Our Lady's Fire is a disease of wheat."

"Yes, that was one of its many names. That was what it was called here in Westphalia. And note that common to all the names I have mentioned is their association with religious ideas. Peasants knew more about the effect of that wheat parasite than the learned world did. The memory of an ancient, vanished wisdom survived among them."

Mist was rising, and trees and shrubs began to disappear in a milk-white haze. Big, slowly falling snow-flakes mingled with the snow dust floating down from the roofs.

"The parasite that we propose to call St Peter's Snow," the baron went on, "is enclosed within the plant and does not completely destroy the activity of the nutritive cells. The part of the plant affected shows hardly any external sign of change. The disease seldom persists more than two or three years in the same area, it dies out, to reappear only many years later. But it migrates, and in doing so generally maintains a definite direction. Only rarely does it spread in several directions simultaneously. The earliest reference to it that I found was in the city chronicle of Perugia for the year 1093, when the whole area between Perugia and Siena was affected. According to the chronicle, in that year seventeen peasants and artisans in the area of Perugia claimed to be prophets and maintained that Christ had appeared to them in the guise of an angel and told them to impose severe penance on the world. They preached, and attracted a large following, and four of them were executed by the sword. A year later the disease appeared in the Verona area, i.e., it had travelled north. Only a few weeks later five thousand persons, nobles and burghers, men, women and children, assembled, forming a terrifying multitude, according to contemporary accounts – and made their way through Lombardy from town to town and church to church, singing penitential psalms, and wherever they went they fell upon priests suspected of loose or worldly living and either killed or maltreated them. That was in 1094, and according to my calculations, St Peter's Snow should have reached Germany a year later, but that did not happen. The fungus seems to have been unable to take the direct route across the Alps, but went round them both east and west and appeared simultaneously a year later in France and Hungary, and in both countries it gave rise to the same uplift of souls, bordering on the miraculous, the visible result of which was the bold venture of the First Crusade and the liberation of the Holy Places."

The baron told me all this with a calm that roused me to violent inner revolt.

"But isn't this theory of yours rather bold?" I said.

He smiled.

"A theory as solidly based as mine, doctor, will not be so easy for you to refute. I have followed the route taken by the wheat parasite through the centuries. I have tracked all its migrations, and I have established that all the great religious movements of the Middle Ages and the modern age – the processions of flagellants, the dance epidemics, the persecution of heretics by Bishop Konrad of Marburg, the Cluniac Church reforms, the Children's Crusade, the so-called Secret Singing of the Upper Rhine, the extermination of the Albigenses in Provence and of the Waldenses in Piedmont, the origin of the cult of St Anne, the Hussite wars, the Anabaptist movement – I have shown that all the religious struggles, all the ecstatic upheavals began in areas in which St Peter's Snow had appeared immediately before. You call it bold theorising, but in every single instance I can produce evidence for my claim."

He opened a drawer of his desk and shut it again. He glanced round the room, obviously looking for the bottle of whisky and the box of cigars that had been left downstairs in the hall. His eyes fell on a Chinese vase on the mantelpiece.

"Look, doctor, China, the country without religion. The Chinese have no religious ideas, only a kind of philosophy. In the Middle Kingdom no grain has been cultivated for thousands of years. Only rice."

He had given up looking for the bottle of whisky and the cigars and rang for the servant.

"And why," I asked, and the question came from my lips of its own accord and without my wanting it to, "why is belief in God disappearing from the world?"

"Belief in God is not disappearing from the world," Baron von Malchin replied. "Only the fervour of belief in God has died out. Why? I too found myself faced with that question, only I stated it differently. To me the problem was this. Had the parasite lost its virulence or wheat its predisposition? One of those two factors had inhibited the development and spread of St Peter's Snow in Europe for more than a century. Well, my laboratory experiments have shown . . ."

There was a knock at the door and the servant appeared, he was the small lad with a slight squint who had fetched me from the station with a sleigh. He remained standing in the doorway.

"What do you want?" the baron said to him. "Rang? No, I didn't ring. I don't want anything, you can go . . . Where was I? Yes, the experiments I have carried out with the aid of my technical assistant have shown that the parasite has lost nothing of its virulence. But the wheat, you see . . ."

He interrupted himself and looked at the door.

"He could have brought me the cigars while he was about it," he went on. "Too stupid, I didn't bring any with me . . . Nowadays the wheat's resistance to the parasite is incomparably greater than it was a hundred years ago. Wheat and rye, like nearly all cultivated crops, come from countries with warmer climates, and so in Europe they are on foreign soil. They were susceptible to the disease as long as they had not adapted to the foreign soil, the process of adaptation lasted for centuries and has now been completed . . . Why hasn't he brought the whisky? I told him to fetch whisky and cigars . . . There's also another factor. The fungus first gains a hold when the plant is in a weak condition, I could give you physiological details about this. But improved conditions of cultivation in our time have resulted in that condition becoming exceptional. St Peter's

Snow has withdrawn to other, wild-growing species which offer it more favourable living conditions, and that, doctor, is the answer to the question why belief in God is disappearing from the world."

After giving me this surprising explanation Baron von Malchin rose and went to the fireplace to warm himself. The wood crackled and the sparks flew, and a narrow tongue of flame shot angrily from between the piled logs as if it were aiming at him.

"That problem, the problem of the predisposition of the wheat, was the decisive one for me. Everything, my plans and my hopes, depended on it. Had I devoted my nights to a fertile idea or sacrificed them to a chimaera? We – my assistant and I – first tried an overdose of the parasite on a healthy plant, and it turned out to be possible to infect young wheat with the germs of the parasite and produce the disease artificially. But that was and remained a laboratory success without any further prospects. For the inoculation was an act of violence that does not occur in nature, and it was only by that act of violence that the plant had been made receptive to the fungus. We soon dropped experimenting on these lines and looked for a way of diminishing or breaking down the plant's resistance. Last year I actually succeeded in producing the disease on a tiny plot of land without inoculation – on damp and insufficiently manured land exposed to the north wind, and above all because I artificially reduced the light. This was perhaps the first time for a century that St Peter's Snow had reappeared in a field of wheat. But it was confined to that small and artificially shaded plot and did not affect a single plant that was exposed to the sun. The experiment was a success and yet a failure. I had found St Peter's Snow, yet all my plans were in ruins. And then, at the time of my deepest depression – and I say this in the presence of three witnesses – my technical assistant came to my aid."

Bibiche looked proudly and with shining eyes first at me and then at the baron. The priest said nothing, but frowned.

The baron turned to the Russian.

97

"Listen, Arkady Fyodorovich," he said. "In your dreamy self-forgetfulness you failed to order cigars. Please send a postcard to the tobacconist, it will be worth while. This is the whole of our supply. It will last for three days at most."

He had lit a cigar and went on: "So that was the situation. Just when I was completely at a loss and did not know which way to turn, this young lady intervened. She had no easy task with me. I am a farmer and I have the head of a farmer, I think only of crops and the soil. But in the end she persuaded me that we had no need of corn or wheatfields, that we could cause the parasite to develop and multiply in an artificial breeding ground, in a liquid medium with quite specific additives. By a process of distillation she succeeded in producing the liquid hallucinogen from the fungus and its spores, and her analysis of the product showed – what did it show, Kallisto?"

"The effective components are a number of alkaloids," Bibiche explained. "There are also small quantities of resinoid products and a little sphacelinic acid, and finally there are traces of an oily substance."

"All that sounds very simple," the baron went on, "but nevertheless it was the work of many months. And now we've reached a stage when we can experiment on a wider basis – no longer restricted to individual objects, doctor. You know that the collective mind has its own laws, it reacts to stimuli differently and more violently . . ."

The priest had risen to his feet, and he wiped his brow with his big, blue-check handkerchief.

"I am an old man who has not got very far in life, and I know you won't listen to me," he said. "But I shall not cease warning you. Don't do it, don't do it here in this village, please, leave my peasants alone, they're badly enough off already. I'm afraid, I tell you. I'm afraid for you, for myself, for all of us. There's always something like disaster in the air in this Westphalian country."

Baron von Malchin shook his head.

"Afraid, my old friend?" he said. "What are you afraid of?

I'm only doing what you have spent your life doing, trying to lead people back to God."

"Do you really know where you are leading them?" the priest asked. "Remember the passage in the Book of Kings: 'He called the corn out of the earth so that the people might eat of it and recognise Him.' And what happened when the people ate of that corn? What does the Book of Kings say?"

"They recognised Him and built altars to Him – the Book of Kings says – and they brought him prisoners to sacrifice to the number of five thousand. And King Ahab sacrificed his own son to him."

"And whom did they recognise?" the priest asked. "To whom did they build altars? To whom did they make human sacrifices?"

"To their god."

"Yes, to their god and not to ours," said the priest. "And their god was Moloch. King Ahab sacrificed his son to Moloch, remember that."

The baron shrugged his shoulders.

"It may be true that King Ahab made human sacrifices to Moloch and not to Jehovah," he said. "But the bloodthirsty god of the Phoenicians is today only the shadow of a memory. Why do you invoke him?"

The priest had reached the doorway, and he turned once more.

"It wasn't I who invoked him," he said. "It was you, but you don't know it yet."

SEVENTEEN

When six o'clock struck I felt an urgent desire to be alone, and I sent away the two people in my waiting room. I gave the woman codliver oil for her child, and the man who complained of neuralgia a sedative and told him to come back next day. He was rather deaf and did not understand me immediately. He complained that the pain in his arm would not go away and said that it came from deep inside and was the result of thick blood, and he wanted me to bleed him, and before I could stop him he had taken off his coat and unbuttoned his shirt. I shouted in his ear that it was too late and that he must come back first thing in the morning, and I told him he would certainly sleep if he took the sedative. Eventually he understood what I was trying to tell him, and he dressed himself and went slowly and clumsily down the stairs, and it was a long time until I heard the door shut behind him.

When I was alone in my room I wondered why I had sent him away. The hours of waiting that lay ahead were bound to pass agonisingly slowly. My meagre preparations were complete. I had bought raspberry sweets in the village shop – they were more confidence-inspiring than the chocolate with soft centres – as well as some apples, a bar of chocolate, a packet of biscuits, dates and a bottle of liqueur – that was all that the shop had to offer. I had put fresh pine branches in the two vases on the mantelpiece, and I now put the worn couch in the corner, where the light did not fall on it, and sprinkled eau de Cologne on the cushions on the two wicker chairs. That was all I could do, and after that there was nothing to do but wait.

I picked up the newspaper and tried to read, but soon discovered that nothing that was happening in the world was capable of rousing my interest and there was nothing capable of distracting me from the single thing round which my thoughts revolved. The result of the elections in South Africa and Argentina, the danger of war in the Far East, the interviews with statesmen, sensational happenings in the Paris courts, parliamentary reports – all those things left me cold. The small advertisements were the only part of the newspaper that engaged my attention to a certain extent. I have often wondered why these minor manifestations of everyday life have such a soothing effect on frayed nerves. Perhaps reading about the needs and wishes of total strangers enables us to forget our own worries and troubles for a short time. A life insurance concern had a vacancy for a supervisor for the Teltow, Jüterbog and Tauch-Belzig districts. The owner of a country house wanted urgently to buy pre-war Persian carpets for cash. Travellers were required for machinery, winter goods, zip fasteners and porcelain ware, and a tall, elegant, attractive lady sought a permanent position as senior saleswoman. I read all these advertisements several times, they gave me a respite from my own troubles by briefly taking me out of my own life and making me feel the cares and wishes of others as if they were my own, and then, when I came back to myself again I almost felt happy, because what I wanted was so little – only that the time would pass more quickly for the next few hours – and by then it was half past six, and Bibiche's arrival was half an hour nearer – and then there was a knock at the door and the landlady came in with my supper.

I ate hurriedly and distractedly, and ten minutes later I could not remember what I had been intending to do. Then it struck me that the smell of food might not disappear from the room in time, so I opened the window and let cold air in.

Outside, mist was creeping up to the roofs, the light over the inn door gleamed gloomily and forlornly through the white haze. While looking out at the street I remembered that I still had a call to make. The wife of a woodworker who lived outside the village was shortly expecting her fifth child. At midday she had complained of violent pains in the small of the back and of weakness when walking, and so I wanted to have another look at her. I shut the window, put two logs on the fire, took my hat and coat and went.

The visit turned out to be unnecessary, as the woman's condition was unchanged, except that her back pains had subsided, and it might be days before the labour pains began. She was in the kitchen, cooking the supper. The sourish odour of the milking pail mingled with the smell of potatoes cooked in their jackets and overcooked pig food. The husband had just come from work, and I chatted with the couple for a while. They were poor, like many in the village. Their only cow had been taken away as security against arrears of tax. Two dark, damp rooms housed a family of eight for whom there were only four beds. Broken window panes and cracks in the doors were plugged with empty sacks. The children came in one after another and cast hungry glances at the potatoes. The woman said that the eldest girl needed a pair of shoes, but unfortunately there was no money in the house.

My aunt had had no use for charity. Everyone must look after himself, and no one helps me, she used to say, and that was the spirit in which she had brought me up. But that evening I felt a need to do a good deed, to help someone, to banish someone's worries. I surreptitiously took five two-mark pieces from my pocket and laid them noiselessly on top of the kitchen stove. Perhaps I did this only because I was fearful for my good fortune that evening and wanted to placate the envy of the gods. The money must have been found immediately after my departure, for I heard the man running down the street behind me, but the mist was so dense that he did not see me, though he was only ten paces away from me.

When I got back my room seemed friendlier, actually almost comfortable. I put two apples on top of the stove to cook them.

Then I turned off all the lights, but the darkness was not complete, because the fire threw a red glow on the worn carpet and the two wicker chairs.

The tailor coughed in his room down below. He was in bed with bronchitis, I had ordered him hot milk with soda water. Otherwise all was quiet, except for the apples sizzling on the stove, and a fine, spicy odour pervaded the room. I sat staring into the fire and did not look at my watch. I did not want to know what the time was and how long I still had to wait.

Suddenly I had an alarming idea. Supposing a visitor arrived. It might be someone whom I could not turn away, someone who insisted on keeping me company, Prince Praxatin, for instance. It was by no means impossible. Praxatin had been here once and stayed till after midnight. What would I do if he walked in and sat down by the fire beside me? The idea that had terrified me for a moment began to amuse me. I imagined him sitting there. I couldn't see him because it was so dark, but there he was, stretching his legs, his head with its flaxen hair cocked slightly to one side, and the wicker chair creaked and complained beneath the weight of his huge body, and the light of the fire was reflected on his highly polished boots.

"Well, Arkady Fyodorovich," I said to the shade in the wicker chair, "you're not very communicative, are you? You've been here for five minutes, but you sit there as silent as an owl in the silence of the night."

"Five minutes?" I made the shadow answer. "I've been here much longer than that, doctor, and I've been watching you, you're impatient, you seem to be waiting for something, and time drags and refuses to pass."

I nodded.

"Yes, time has two shoes," the shade went on. "One limps with painful slowness and the other leaps ahead, and to-day in this room time is wearing its limping shoe, it refuses to budge."

"Quite right, Arkady Fyodorovich," I sighed. "That is exactly how slowly the hours pass."

"I see you're not used to waiting, doctor, that's bad. I have learned to wait. When I came here, I said to myself: Well, how long will the Reds last in Russia? A year, or perhaps two, I assured myself, and waited. But now, after all these years, I know that no time-limit has been imposed on them. They're there for all eternity, and I'm waiting in vain. Are you waiting in vain, doctor?"

"No," I replied shortly and sharply.

"In that case you're waiting for a woman, I thought as much straight away," said the Russian. "Of course. I should have realised it at once. Dim lighting, apples, chocolate, a box of something, even dates, as well as some liqueur. All that's missing is roses."

He put his hand to his mouth and coughed.

"There ought to be a Delft vase on the table with white roses, don't you think so, doctor?" he went on.

"Stop it, Arkady Fyodorovich," I said irritably. "What business is it of yours?"

"No roses, then, for all I care, don't be angry with me," said the voice in the wicker chair in soft, singing tones. "Why have real roses in any case? They're utterly conventional flowers, completely lacking in character, and you're expecting her without any. Just imagine it. In this God-forsaken village, this wilderness, you're expecting a woman. Even chickens lay eggs for lucky men. There is of course one woman here who's as lovely and slender as Our Lady, and her skin is as white as apple blossom, and when she speaks it's like the wind moving over the earth in spring. Is it she whom you're waiting for, doctor?"

"Perhaps," I replied.

He had another fit of coughing, and pulled his chair a little nearer the fire.

"Then you're waiting in vain," he said. "She won't turn up. I too waited for a whole year, and she never turned up."

"I can well believe she didn't come and see you," I said, and laughed, and I was surprised at how spiteful and malicious my laughter sounded.

"And you think she'll turn up for you?" he replied. "Perhaps she will, we'll see. I'm interested in seeing what happens. I'm prepared to be convinced. I'll stay and wait with you."

"You intend to stay?" I exclaimed. "What an idea. You're going home, you're ill, you've got a cough."

"Not likely. I'm not going to die of this cough. What time are you expecting her?"

"Arkady Fyodorovich," I said severely, "enough is enough. You're *de trop* here, you're going, and you're going right away. I know for certain that you're going now."

He did not move from his wicker chair. The fire flickered, and for a moment I seemed to see his face.

"Oh? Are you sure of that? Are you threatening me, by any chance? You won't get anywhere with that, it would be like trying to fell a tree with a bunch of twigs. What do you propose to threaten me with, doctor?"

"I'm not threatening you, Arkady Fyodorovich," I said. "You will go now, if for no other reason than that you're a gentleman."

"Yes," the Russian said after a short pause. "As a gentleman I certainly ought to go. But don't you sometimes feel a barbed hook in your soul? Don't you feel it now? To tell you the truth, I'm jealous. I'm sick with jealousy, I'm suffering the tortures of the damned. I ought to go and I've got to stay. I've got to find out who the woman is."

"Arkady Fyodorovich, pull yourself together," I said to him. "You're not being serious. You're not jealous, and you have no cause for jealousy. Go home quietly, I'm not expecting the woman you're talking about."

"Oh, if only you were telling the truth," he said with a sigh. "But you're not telling the truth, I can see it in your eyes. Listen, I'm going to propose something to you. We're men, aren't we, civilised human beings, outcasts in this wilderness, but civilised human beings all the same. We'll settle this matter fairly and without quarrelling. I have a pack of cards here. Who picks the higher card stays, and the other one goes and doesn't come back. Do you agree?"

"You mean a duel? An American duel?"

"Why do you call it a duel? I didn't say the loser must immediately put a bullet through his head. All he has to do is to go and not come back. A duel? Just a little game with modest stakes, that's all."

"You call that modest stakes? Very well, I agree. But it's too dark, I can't see the cards. Wait while I turn on the light."

"No, don't," he exclaimed. "What for? It's quite unnecessary. You're just as jealous as I am, and jealousy has cat's eyes. We can both see very well in the dark. I'm now going to draw a card . . . I've drawn the knave of spades. Now it's your turn."

"I can't see anything, so it looks as if I'm not jealous," I said with a laugh. "But I don't think you like light very much. And I bet that if I now switch on the light you'll have vanished. So I'll now switch it on, at the risk of putting an end to our little conversation."

"Switch it on, then," he called out, "try switching it on, you won't manage it, there's a short circuit, doctor, a short circuit."

"The devil take it," I exclaimed, "that's the last straw."

I tried to find the switch, but couldn't, I upset a chair and struck my forehead against the bookcase. "Don't waste your time, there's a short circuit," the Russian said and laughed, and his laugh turned into a fit of coughing. Then I found the switch and there was light in the room.

I stretched, and put my hand to my aching forehead. The light dazzled me.

"Have you gone, Arkady Fyodorovich?" I called out and looked round the room. "What a pity, now you'll never find out who's coming to see me this evening. Why were you suddenly in such a hurry? Leaving like this without saying goodbye? I'm surprised at you, those are not the manners of a man of the world. Well, then, good night, sleep well, don't think too much about . . ."

I stopped. The church clock began to strike. I stood still and counted the strokes, it was nine o'clock.

EIGHTEEN

Nine o'clock had struck, and there was no sign of her. I opened the window and leaned out – all was quiet, there were no light footsteps, there was no crunching in the snow, no shadow gliding through the mist. Why isn't she coming? I wondered in dismay. What had happened, for heaven's sake, what could have happened? It struck me that I didn't have a lemon, I'd thought of everything except a lemon for the tea. The shop was shut, I should have to go across to the inn – but what for? She wasn't coming, so what for? Perhaps she has been here and found the door bolted. I'd told the landlady . . . But I should have gone down myself to make sure the front door was unlocked. Why hadn't I done it?

I dashed downstairs in such a hurry that I forgot to shut the window. No, the front door was not locked. Slowly I went upstairs again, the cold air rushed to meet me, and I looked out at the street again before shuttering the window.

I poured myself out a glass of brandy and noticed that my hand was trembling. Keep calm, keep calm, I said to myself, and sat down and considered. What had happened? She must have forgotten. She was in her laboratory, concentrating on her work, and had forgotten the day and the time. Perhaps she had been tired, had lain on the divan for a rest and gone to sleep. Or perhaps she had just not wanted to come. Does one keep a rash, over-hasty promise? What for? What did I mean to her? Do you think I could bear life here without you? she had said. But that had been two days ago, and in two days so much can change in a woman.

Once more I helped myself to some brandy – it was my third. I wanted to go on drinking till the bottle was empty, till Bibiche and the whole world was indifferent to me. But perhaps I was being unfair to her, perhaps she had not forgotten, perhaps something had cropped up at the last moment, perhaps the baron had sent for her, or had met her on the way here. Another brandy. Your health, Bibiche, though you didn't turn up, I still love you all the same, damn it, I can't help it. If I see you in the morning . . . Perhaps she's unwell, perhaps she's in bed with a temperature. But then she would have let me know, through the small boy who came here before. You're angry with me, and I don't know why. Poor Bibiche, that's what the note said last time. What will she write today? You mustn't wait for me any longer. Did you really think I'd come? He'll be here at any moment. Good evening, the young lady sent you this. Another brandy, it does you good. All night I'll . . .

There was a knock at the door.

There he is. That's the small boy, with a note from her. She's ill, no, she isn't. She doesn't want to come. Yes, she does, but she can't, the baron's there. Come in, I called out huskily and turned away, I didn't want to see.

"Good evening," said Bibiche. "Oh, what a lovely smell of cooked apples, how nice, I adore them. Well? I haven't kept you waiting long, have I?"

I looked at her, she was standing in the open doorway in her coat and snow shoes. I glanced at my watch, it was three minutes past nine.

She held out her hand for me to kiss.

"Really, I'm amazed at how punctual I am, it's not like me at all. So this is how you live. I've often wondered what your room looked like."

I helped her out of her coat.

"Don't look round, Bibiche," I said, and my heart beat. "It's so depressing here. The room . . ."

She laughed, and she had a special way of laughing, with her eyes and nostrils.

"Yes," she said, "one can tell you haven't had many lady friends here. Or have you, perhaps? Ladies from Breda? Or from Osnabrück? The light's a bit too harsh. You can turn it off, the table lamp will do . . . yes, that's better."

I put the tea urn on the table and lit the spirit lamp. We were both embarrassed, but neither wanted the other to notice it.

"Is it cold outside?" I asked for the sake of saying something.

"Yes. That's to say, I don't know. Perhaps it is. I didn't notice. I hurried, I was afraid."

"Afraid?"

"Yes, really. I was very stupid. When I shut the front door behind me I felt very cheerful, but then . . . Walking here in the dark. That's when I got frightened. The short walk became so terrifyingly long."

"I shouldn't have let you come alone."

She shrugged her shoulders.

"And I'm still frightened now. Are you sure no one can come in? Supposing a patient . . ."

"That's not very likely at this time of day," I said. "And if anybody did come, he'd pull the bell downstairs and I wouldn't let him in."

She lit herself a cigarette.

"We'll have a cup of tea and a chat and then I'll go," she said.

I said nothing. She looked at the blue flame of the spirit lamp. The tailor downstairs had one of his coughing fits.

She started.

"Who's that?" she asked.

"That's my landlord. He has slight bronchitis."

"Will he go on like that all night?" she wanted to know.

"No. If he doesn't go to sleep, I'll go down and give him a codeine or something."

Something seemed to have upset her.

"I don't really know why I came," she said. "Can you tell me, by any chance? Yes, look at me, have a good look at me. What do you expect? Do you expect me to fling my arms round you? You haven't even said good evening to me properly."

I bent over her and put my arms round her shoulders. But she wouldn't let me kiss her, and pushed me away.

"Bibiche," I exclaimed. I was surprised and rather hurt.

"Yes, I'm Bibiche," she said with a laugh, "still the same Bibiche. How clumsy you are. You've torn my dress. Have you any blue cotton, by any chance? No? Why should you have any blue cotton?"

I offered to go down to the tailor's and ask him for some blue cotton.

"Yes, do," she said. "But don't be away for long. I'm frightened, yes, really frightened when I'm alone. I'll lock the door behind you. When you come back you'll have to knock and say it's you, or I shan't let you in."

When I came back the door was not locked.

She was standing in front of the mirror, tidying her hair. Her dress was on the divan. A red embroidered kimono was flung loosely round her shoulders, I had not noticed she had brought it with her. The mirror reflected her lovely, calm, determined face.

"Well," she said, without turning towards me. "Now you can say good evening to me."

I took her head between my hands and bent it back. She let out a little cry of pain, perhaps I had been too violent. Then we found each other in a painfully violent kiss.

"You came here and disturbed my peace," she said at last when I released her lips. "It's in your eyes. Do you always find it so easy with women? When you look at one . . . Do you really love me?"

"Can't you tell, Bibiche?"

"Yes, but I want to hear you say it. No, don't say it, tell me where you were living during the whole year when we didn't see each other. Did you have a girl? Was she prettier than me? Yes? No? Really no? But you don't have to stop kissing me, one can answer and kiss at the same time, or can't one?"

She shut her eyes and let me kiss her, she let the kimono slip from her shoulders, and a shudder of joy went through me when I held her in my arms like that.

She left me in the morning, when it began to get light. She would not let me come with her. We said goodbye in the dark corner between the staircase and the door of the tailor's workshop.

"Yes, I'll come again soon," she said, snuggling up to me. "No, not tomorrow, we have a great deal of work in the next few days, but when it's finished I shan't keep you waiting. I should so much like to stay, but I can't, I've got to go and save the cup of milk, or pussy'll lap it up. No, silly, I haven't got a cat, that's a nursery rhyme. If I meet anyone I'll say I've been for a walk. Will they believe me? I don't mind if they don't. Kiss me again. And how do you know they called me Bibiche when I was a child? Did I tell you? We must see each other again today. Knock at my window when you pass. Another kiss. And now . . ."

I watched her going away, with short, careful footsteps through the snow. She turned once and waved to me. When she disappeared I went up to my room. There was a kind of joyful restlessness in me, a feeling I had never known before. I felt I must immediately start something completely new, such as learning to ride or embarking on some sort of scientific work, or at least taking an hour's walk alone through the snow.

At nine o'clock my day began, my usual day, just as if nothing had happened overnight. The first patient arrived. He was the man with neuralgia whom I had sent away the evening before because I was expecting Bibiche, and now that she had gone he had turned up again. I greeted him with real pleasure, as if he were an old friend. "Well, tell me, what sort of night did you have?" I said, and offered him a cigar, biscuits, dates and a glass of liqueur.

NINETEEN

During the next few days I did not manage to see Bibiche alone. Whenever I passed the priest's house Baron von Malchin was with her in the laboratory. When I looked through the window I could see his narrow head with its high forehead and greying temples in the light of the lamp, or he would be holding a test tube, or standing with Bibiche in front of a cylindrical glass vessel that looked like a Soxhlet apparatus. Once the laboratory was dark and Bibiche was sitting at the typewriter in the next room and he appeared to be walking up and down and dictating to her – I could not see him, but I saw his shadow gliding along the wall and the floor.

He was always with her, but I was no longer upset by her having no time for me. The night she had spent with me had changed a great deal in me. If previously I had been ill, now I felt well again. The doubts that had tormented me had gone, and I was no longer at the mercy of ever-changing moods. I loved Bibiche even more than before, I loved her as I love her now, but there was now a great peace inside me, I felt like a rock climber who has climbed a steep wall with much toil and danger and is now lying supremely happily in the sun at the top, full of self-confidence. So the waiting was easy to put up with. I should see her again as soon as she had finished her work, and when I felt lonely in my room and longed for her, my thoughts flew back to that night.

Also I now had more work. There were two cases of diphtheria in the village, and I was worried by little Elsie's condition. She had got over her scarlet fever. The rash had gone, but the frail organism was weakened, the child needed a change of air, a longish stay in a less raw climate seemed to me to be indicated, and I wanted to discuss this with the baron, whose plans left him so little time for his small daughter.

I was coming from the forester's lodge, it was a Saturday, just a week has passed since then. Last week, then, I walked down the village street, looking for the baron. The villagers were standing about in small groups outside the Stag inn and the shop. Men, women and children, everyone who was not at home peeling potatoes was there. The peasants were silent, as usual, but on their lined and weather-beaten faces there was something like restless expectation. They were watching a sleigh loaded with beer barrels which was advancing slowly towards the manor house, and the driver was walking beside it, cracking his whip. The shopkeeper immediately told me without being asked that the baron had invited the whole village to celebrate his name-day on the estate. The farmers and tenants were to be entertained in the garden room in the manor house and the farm-hands and woodcutters in the servants' hall on the ground floor of the administrative building. The menu was to be roast pork and sausages with sauerkraut, and there were to be two glasses of schnapps for everyone, and as much beer as they liked. The baron had also ordered from him, the shopkeeper, a whole crate of gingerbread to be distributed as a treat for the children. The shopkeeper said that the baron had never before been so generous.

"The peasants say that to celebrate the occasion he intends to waive some peasants' arrears of rent, but that I don't believe," he said. "How would that be consistent with law and order? I know the baron, he sympathises with the poor but, so far as rent is concerned, he doesn't allow himself to be trifled with. Law and order must be maintained, and what would happen to the world if they weren't? If people once discovered it was possible to monkey around with the rent . . . What's the matter, my little man, why the hurry? Where's the fire? Thirty pfennigs-worth of tobacco for grandpa? Here you are, don't lose it, and my kindest regards to grandpa, and be careful not to knock down the church tower in your excitement."

These last remarks were directed at a small boy who had been impatiently tapping on the counter with a coin to interrupt the shopkeeper's flow of talk.

It was dark in the laboratory and in the room next door. I knocked at the window, but nothing happened. I knocked again and louder, but nobody came and opened the door and all was quiet. An unpleasant feeling went through me. Bibiche had always been in the laboratory at this time of day. Had she gone away? Had the baron sent her to Berlin again by any chance? Was she perhaps again driving the green Cadillac through the station square at Osnabrück? No, that's impossible, I assured myself, she would not have gone without letting me know. After all that had passed between us, she would not have gone without saying goodbye. Had she finished her work, perhaps? Had she succeeded in making the preparation odourless? The smell had been revolting, it had made me feel quite sick. But now they had reached the stage when they could experiment on a bigger scale – of course – the whole village had been invited to the manor house this evening. Two glasses of schnapps for everyone and as much beer as they liked. It wouldn't be in the beer because, if everyone drank as much as he liked, exact dosing would be impossible, so it would be in the schnapps. The hallucinogen that Bibiche had distilled from Our Lady's Fire would be in the schnapps the peasants would drink, and perhaps the church would be full of praying peasants tomorrow, so why was the priest so opposed to it? And tomorrow Bibiche would be coming, as she had promised. When the work's finished I shan't keep you waiting, she had said.

I had reached the manor house. There was no one about whom I could ask where the baron was. The whole staff were presumably busy with preparations in the garden room or the administrative building. The dim light of the lamp fell on two persons sitting silently facing each other in two carved wooden armchairs. One of them rose when I entered, and I recognised the priest.

"Good evening, doctor," he said. "Are you looking for the baron? He's sitting there, fast asleep – he was actually fast asleep when I came in. I wanted to talk to him too. You can come closer, you won't wake him. He's sleeping the sleep of the just."

I shut the door noiselessly behind me and tiptoed towards the baron. He was sitting leaning forward with his head resting on his arm, and his breathing was quiet and even. An open book was on the table in front of him. He had dropped off reading Lucian.

"Isn't it extraordinary that he can sleep so quietly?" said the priest. "Isn't it amazing that there should be no trace of anxiety, concern or doubt in the dreams of a man who has assumed such a heavy responsibility?"

"But reverend father," I said quietly and diffidently, "are you unwilling to share the responsibility with him? Aren't all his plans for the benefit of the Church of Christ?"

"No," he replied, softly but resolutely. "The Church of Christ has nothing to do with what this man has in mind. Man is on earth to worship God of his own free will. Don't you know that?"

I said nothing. There was no sound in the hall but that of the baron's gentle breathing.

"Then why, reverend father, did you not forbid your flock to come here?"

"I thought of doing so," he replied, "but it would have been useless, they would have come all the same. They don't listen to me."

"If no error has crept into this man's plans," I said, "from now on the peasants of Morwede will listen to you."

The priest looked at me, and then looked past me at the sleeper in the armchair.

"Do you think so?" he then said. "Do you know the people

116

here? You are a young man, doctor, do you know people at all? I have grown old among my peasants and woodcutters, I know their cares and their thoughts, their wants and their wishes, I know what goes on secretly in their minds, and I'm afraid."

He pointed to the baron.

"Look," he said. "I came here to talk to him yet again. Perhaps, I said to myself, at the very last moment I may succeed in making him see the dreadful nature of the responsibility he is assuming, and persuading him to change his mind. But I have been sitting facing him and watched him sleeping for half an hour. If a tremor of unrest had crossed his face, if he had moaned in his dreams . . . But you see how quietly he sleeps. A man who sleeps as quietly as that an hour before the decisive step is taken will heed no warning. I have no more to say to him. I'm going. Good night."

I went too. I went down the spiral staircase to look for Bibiche.

TWENTY

In the small drawing room in which Baron von Malchin used to take his after-dinner coffee and read the newspaper I found Prince Praxatin and Federico. They were sitting at the card table. When I walked in Praxatin nodded to me familiarly if somewhat absently and took no further notice of me, but Federico looked fixedly over the cards at me. He knew I had come from the forester's lodge. Normally I would have told him something about little Elsie, that she was a little better, or had asked after him, or something of the sort, but this time I said nothing. I had been going to advise the baron to send her to a sunnier clime, but now this suddenly struck me as being, not an essential medical step in the necessity of which I believed, but a terrible let-down to Federico. Those big, iris-blue eyes which looked at me inquiringly made me feel uncertain. I avoided them and pretended to take an interest in a game of cards.

I don't know what they were playing, but I soon noticed that it was not going the way the Russian wanted, for he looked more and more disgruntled and accompanied the successive phases of the game with exclamations in Russian and German.

He suddenly flung the cards on the table.

"I don't understand," he exclaimed. "Yesterday, Federico, you couldn't win a single game against me, and today you're playing quite differently, you're suddenly playing like a master. You even use tricks that I didn't teach you, and I've already had to give you back the IOU you gave me yesterday. You're not playing the game, Federico, now stop looking at the doctor and look me in the face. Tell me the truth. Who taught you these tricks?"

"Nobody did," Federico replied. "I've been thinking overnight about how to play to beat you."

"You've been thinking about it overnight?" the Russian exclaimed angrily. "But you shouldn't think, it's taking an unfair advantage, you have no right to do it. The fox pretends to be asleep, but actually it's counting the chickens. That's not fair, Federico. It's not usual among gentlemen to think and work out tricks in secret."

"I didn't know that," said Federico.

The Russian turned to me.

"Perhaps you suppose, doctor," he said while shuffling the cards and dealing them again, "that I play cards with Federico for my own pleasure, to pass the time or even, perhaps, to win money. Such a supposition would be totally mistaken, doctor. I have undertaken the task of forming his mind and leading him towards the great problems that alone satisfy the intellect, for I have a great love of philosophy, doctor, I think continually about the most difficult problems, such as the boundaries of infinite space, for instance. That problem occupies me night and day. But before setting about my task, doctor, I must introduce Federico to the laws of logical thought, and for that purpose I use card-playing. I play with him every day, and devote a great deal of time to it. I do this with an eye on the development of his character. My objective is to make him so fed up with cards that in a year, perhaps, he will be so sick of them that he will no longer be able to stand the sight of them. I am teaching him to abhor all card games, and thus to avoid dangers that I myself did not always escape. When I think of my past life I feel sad, doctor. Anything lost can be found again, what is irrecoverable is wasted time. I also combine these lessons with some practice in French conversation."

When he had finished dealing the cards he said to Federico: "*Mais vous êtes dans les nuages, mon cher. À quoi songez-vous? Prenez vos cartes, s'il vous plaît. Vous êtes le premier à jouer.*"

Federico picked up the cards, but put them down again.

"You look as if you had something to tell me, doctor," he said.

I shook my head.

"Or as if there was something you didn't want to tell me. You're keeping something from me, doctor."

His anxious, inquiring eyes embarrassed me.

"I intended to postpone telling you," I began. "I was going to tell you tomorrow. But as you ask me . . . I think it necessary for little Elsie . . ."

He seemed to have guessed what I was going to say. His expression of anxious tension gave way to hatred, hatred of a kind I had never before seen on a human face. It frightened me, the boy's eyes turned me into a coward.

"I consider there is no further need for little Elsie to remain in isolation," I corrected myself. "I no longer have any objection to your going to see her."

He gazed at me. First he looked mistrustful, then surprised, then thunderstruck, then radiant.

"I can go and see her?" he exclaimed. "You allow me to? And I thought you were my enemy. You release me from my promise? Thank you. Shake hands. Thank you. I'll go straight away."

"Don't go now," I said. "She's asleep. You'll wake her."

"No, I shan't. Don't worry. I'll go into her room quite quietly and creep out again quite quietly. I shan't even breathe. I only want to see her."

A shadow flitted across his face.

"You won't tell my father?"

"No. I shan't give you away."

"You know – if my father found out – he has already threatened to send her to Switzerland or England. But I couldn't live without her."

"Oh, you could," said the Russian. "You could quite definitely live without her."

"I shan't tell your father," I promised, and abandoned the

120

idea of sending the sick child to the Mediterranean. She'll get better here, I assured myself, the forest air may do her good, and in a few weeks it will be spring.

Federico turned to the Russian.

"I'm going now, Arkady Fyodorovich. You heard, the doctor has released me from my promise," he said. "Goodbye, I'm sorry I made you angry. I'll give you a return game tomorrow."

He went, and the Russian looked at him angrily. Then he started rebuking me.

"Did you have to tell him that while we were playing?" he said. "You really could have waited. What on earth is there to do now? Absolutely nothing. It's eight o'clock. There's nothing for it but to go down and look after our guests."

I went down to the hall, and found Bibiche there. She was alone. She jumped up and took me by the wrists, which was a gesture peculiar to her.

"Where have you been?" she exclaimed. "I've been looking for you all day. Have you been thinking about me at all? You don't care for me one little bit any longer, do you? Well, what are you waiting for? Do I have to ask you for a kiss? Thank you, that's very kind of you. Yes, you may kiss me again. He's gone downstairs, but I'll make it up with him again."

I did not at first realise that she was talking about the baron. "I've been quarrelling with him," she went on. "A very serious quarrel. With whom? The baron, of course, about the hallucinogen. He maintained that we two, he and I, should not take it, but I disagreed. We were the leaders, he said, we must remain clear-headed and dispassionate and be above things, our task was to lead and not be carried away. That's what the quarrel was about. I said that being above it meant being out of it, and just because he was the leader he must feel and think what the crowd thought and felt. I couldn't persuade him, and he couldn't persuade me. He was a bit upset when he left me."

"So you're going to take the hallucinogen, Bibiche?" I said.

"Come and sit down," she said, and dragged me to the

fireside bench. "Darling, I've taken it already. If you want to warn me, it's too late, I had to take it. Please understand me. I'm not a very happy person, you see, and perhaps it's because I lost my faith, and I want to be able to pray again as I prayed when I was a child. Since they shot my father – you don't know about that? Haven't I told you? When they proclaimed a republic in Greece – no, he wasn't killed in street fighting, he was legally convicted and shot. He was aide-de-camp to the King. We could hear the volley and the roll of drums from the house we were living in. Since that day I haven't prayed. I've believed in science and not in God, and I want to be able to pray again, I want my childhood faith back. Do you understand now?"

For a while we were both silent. She leaned against me.

"I went to your room today, do you realise that?" she said suddenly. "I went there to look for you, and I sat alone in your room. I had promised you I'd come as soon as the work was finished. I was frightened, but in spite of that I went up to your room and waited. Your landlord still has that cough. Why does your room smell of chloroform, it makes one quite tired. With the fire in the grate and everything so quiet I nearly went to sleep. And where were you? You kept *me* waiting. Did you look for me here? You looked for me everywhere except in your own lodgings, that's very funny."

She threw her head back and laughed, she laughed with her eyes and her nostrils.

"No, I shan't come this evening," she went on. "I'm rather tired, you see, I'm going home soon. Don't look so upset. I'll be there tomorrow. At nine o'clock? No, earlier, much earlier. As soon as it's dark. There'll be a knock at the door and Bibiche will be there. You might make sure you're alone. But tomorrow's Sunday. You didn't know that tomorrow's Sunday? Tell me, what world are you living in? One can tell that you're happy. It's only in dreams or when one's happy that one doesn't know what day of the week it is."

★

122

Late that evening I went back to the manor house.

I went into the big garden room, which was over-heated. Thick clouds of tobacco smoke made my eyes smart, and there was a smell of beer and of food that had got cold and of too many people. The sound of an accordion came from somewhere, and the peasants sitting over their beer were talking rather more loudly than usual, and now and again a joke I did not understand would go round the table. The women wanted to go home. My landlord the tailor and another man whom he introduced as his brother-in-law came up to me and insisted on our drinking each other's health.

I didn't see the baron, but I saw Prince Praxatin. It was he who was playing the accordion. He was sitting on an empty beer barrel, and he was playing to an audience of peasants' wives, who watched him in non-comprehending amazement, a Russian song, the song of the Black Hussars going into battle. He was the only one who had had too much to drink.

TWENTY-ONE

Next day I stayed at home, and when it began to get dark I put down the book I was reading. I was not impatient, I was sure Bibiche was coming, and I enjoyed the pleasure of waiting and the slight tremor of excitement inside me as one enjoys a sweet fruit or an expensive, mature claret. The time passed – let it pass, I said to myself, some time soon, when it's dark, there'll be a knock at the door, and Bibiche will be there.

But when does it get really dark? I wondered. I could still distinguish the chair and table and mirror and wardrobe in my room, I could even make out the Shakespearean figures of the heliograph on the wall, the king, the jester, the woman appealing for the king's aid, and the exotic ambassador and his retinue. So it wasn't quite dark yet. I spent some time looking at the picture – then the outlines grew indistinct and I could make out only the king and the jester, and they grew indistinct too, though the gilt frame now stood out distinctly from the wall and the picture plane, so it still wasn't quite dark yet.

I did not look at my watch – it made no difference what the time was, after all. By now it might be six o'clock or even seven – no, it could not be seven, because my landlady always brought me my supper between half-past six and seven. I was not hungry, and I lay on the sofa and smoked, and by this time it was so dark that I could not see the cigarette smoke.

It's dark, Bibiche, I said to myself, quite loudly. It had been dark for a long time. If you come now nobody'll see you. And now you must come, do you hear me? You must. I want you to. You mustn't keep me waiting any longer, do you hear me?

I clenched my teeth and held my breath and tried to concentrate on the idea that Bibiche must come now, this very instant I ordered her to. Then I shut my eyes and thought I could see her coming out of the priest's house in response to my will and making her way with small, timid footsteps along the snowy village street. No, I shouldn't have done that, I said to myself, she should come of her own free will. I was certain, absolutely certain, that she was going to knock at the door before another minute had passed. No, there was no need for her to knock. I opened the door, I wanted to hear her light footsteps on the creaking wooden stairs, and while I stood there listening and waiting for the footsteps that didn't come the church clock struck.

So it was six o'clock. It couldn't be seven yet, or the supper would have been here by now. Or was my landlady late for the first time? I hadn't counted the strokes. I turned on the light and looked at my watch.

I had a shock. It was eight o'clock.

It's strange, but for a moment I thought only of my landlady, it was on her account I had a shock. What could have happened to her, I wondered. Why hadn't she come? But did that matter, I said to myself. What do I care about the tailor's wife? Bibiche, where's Bibiche? Why isn't she here? What has happened to Bibiche?

Only now did I feel fear, real fear.

Bibiche had taken the hallucinogen, and who knew what side effects it might have? There had been no experiments with it, or rather there had been one, and I had wrecked it. It's my fault if something has happened to her. Perhaps she's ill, some sort of heart condition, she's calling out and nobody can hear, she needs me and I'm not there.

A moment later I was down in the street. It was then the motorcyclist incident occurred. The vision of the man driving down the village street with two dead hares slung over his back and jumping off his machine outside the inn was the first thing that came back to me after my return to consciousness. I dodged him, and fell. Where did he get the hares from, I wondered as I got to my feet, because it was the close season for hares and partridges, and I noticed that I was still holding my watch. I'd broken the glass when I fell. I put it in my pocket and hurried on.

The laboratory door was open, and I went in. The rooms were dark and ice-cold. I turned on the light. Bibiche was not there.

I breathed a sigh of relief. Bibiche wasn't ill, she'd gone out. A slight hope rose in me. Perhaps she's at my place, I said to myself, she may have got there just after I left – yesterday she was waiting there while I was looking for her everywhere else.

I hurried back, and then went slowly up the stairs, with my heart beating, but taking my time. I gently opened the door, wanting to surprise her.

She wasn't there. The room was as I'd left it, only the fire had gone out.

And now grief broke in on me, I no longer believed she would be coming, something had happened that made her unable to keep her promise. But what? What could it have been?

And while I stood there, shivering in front of the burnt-out fire and full of gloomy thoughts, I suddenly had an idea.

Bibiche is in church, I said to myself. Of course she's in church, why didn't I think of that before? She took the hallucinogen and has recovered her faith, she's praying to God for the first time in years. She's kneeling on the cold stone tiles between peasants who have taken the hallucinogen like her and are either in a state of ecstatic rapture or are obsessed with the fear of hell, and the church is filled with the swelling notes of the organ, and the priest is blessing one and all and saying the Ave Maria, and her soul is one with God.

I dashed to the church. I was struck by how empty the street was, I did not meet a single person on my way. The church was in darkness and all was quiet, not an organ note was to be heard. I pushed open the heavy door and went in.

The church was empty.

For a moment I stood there in amazement. I had never seen the church as deserted as this. But then I reminded myself that it was half-past eight, Vespers were just over. But where was Bibiche? She wasn't at home, she wasn't at church, where could she be?

At the manor house, I answered myself, with the baron, they've been quarrelling, he's upset, and now she has a chance of making it up with him, and that's why she didn't come to me.

Snow had started to drift, short, violent gusts of icy wind came whistling into my face. I turned up my coat collar and struggled on through the snow and the wind. A week had passed since then, and on that Sunday, February 24th, I made my way to Baron von Malchin's house for the last time.

I met only one person on the way. I recognised him, he was the man with neuralgia. He was going to walk straight past me, but I stopped him.

"Where are you going?" I called out. "Were you wanting me, by any chance?"

He shook his head.

"I'm going to hear the preaching," he called out.

"The preaching?" I replied. "Where is there preaching this evening?"

"They're preaching everywhere in the village. They're preaching for the poor. At the baker's, the blacksmith's, and at the Stag inn. I'm going to the Stag."

"Go, then, and take good care of yourself, make sure you don't get cold," I called out to him. "And enjoy the beer at the Stag."

"Yes, I'm going," he answered and tramped off through the snow.

I found Baron von Malchin in the hall of the manor house. Bibiche was not there.

TWENTY-TWO

Baron von Malchin was sitting alone in the hall. The day he had been waiting for so long had come. He had looked forward to it calmly, and even now he showed no sign of excitement. A half-empty bottle of whisky was in front of him, he had a cigar in his hand, and clouds of blue smoke rose towards the ceiling.

He asked after Prince Praxatin, whom he had not seen all day, but I could not enlighten him. Bibiche was not here either – where could she be? But I could not bring myself to ask him. With a brief, almost peremptory gesture he pointed to a chair. I wanted to go, but could not. In his presence I felt the greatness of the hour and had to stay.

He began to speak. Once more he unfolded before my eyes the tremendous, soaring Gothic edifice of his plans and hopes, and I listened enthralled by the boldness of his ideas. The whisky bottle was emptied and the clouds of cigar smoke grew denser, but he went on talking about the Emperor of the true blood and the new Empire that must arise in spite of all the false hopes and opinions of men.

"And Federico?" I asked, and inexplicable misgivings suddenly made me shudder. "Does he know of the task awaiting him? Does he feel up to it? And will he be up to it?"

A gleam came into Baron von Malchin's eyes.

"I have taught him what Frederick taught his son Manfred," he said. "I have taught him about the nature of the world, the making of the body and the creation of the soul, the transience of matter and the immutability of eternal things. I have taught him how to live among men and yet over them. But the secret lies in the dynastic blood. Those who have sprung from the true blood are granted the knowledge that we others can only glimpse at or acquire with great difficulty. He is the third Frederick promised by the Sibyls. He will transform the age and alter its laws."

"And you?" I asked. "What will your function be in the age of transformation?"

A remote smile appeared on his lips.

"To him I shall be what Peter was to the Saviour, a humble fisherman, but always at his side," he replied.

He rose to his feet and listened.

"Do you hear the bells?" he said. "Yes? Do you hear them? The peasants are in the church, forming themselves into a procession. Now they will be coming, singing the old hymns to the Virgin Mary as in my grandfather's time."

I heard the bells. The church is empty, the church is empty, each stroke tolled, and each was like a hammer-blow to my heart, and inside me was a great fear that grew with every stroke until it became intolerable and I felt my heart was going to break.

A gust of cold air swept through the room. The baron looked over my head towards the door.

"You?" he exclaimed in amazement. "What do you want of me? I didn't expect you at this time of day."

I turned. The schoolmaster was standing in the doorway.

"Are you still here, baron?" he panted. "I hurried here as fast as I could. Why haven't you gone yet? Don't you know what is happening outside?"

"Yes, I do," said Baron von Malchin. "The bells are ringing and the peasants are coming here in procession and singing their hymns to the Virgin Mary."

"Hymns to the Virgin Mary?" the schoolmaster shrieked. "Yes, the bells are ringing, but they are ringing the alarm, and the peasants are singing, not hymns to the Virgin Mary, but the Internationale. They want to burn down the roof over your head, baron."

The baron looked at him and said nothing.

"What are you waiting for?" the schoolmaster yelled at him. "Your tenants are coming, baron, your tenants are coming with scythes and flails. We've never been friends, baron, but now your life is at stake. Yes, your life's at stake. Why do you stand there like that? Get your car out of the garage and get away fast."

"It's too late for that," we heard the priest say. "They've surrounded the house and won't let you out."

The priest came down the staircase on Federico's arm. His cassock was in tatters, and the big blue check handkerchief that he held pressed to his cheek was stained with blood. Wild shouts and cries came from the park and the street.

"They attacked and beat me," said the priest, "and women were among them. They dragged me away and locked me in a barn. But then they didn't trouble about me any longer and I managed to escape."

Where's Bibiche? was the thought that flashed through my mind. I must find her, for heaven's sake. She's outside alone with the raging peasants.

"Let me out. I must find her," I yelled at the schoolmaster, but he took no notice of me.

"If only I'd had time to release the dogs," the baron said. He produced his revolver and laid it in front of him on the table. Federico stood silently by his side. He had the huge Saracen sword in his hands – he must have fetched that totally useless weapon from the baron's study upstairs.

"I implore you not to shoot, baron," the priest called out. "Listen to them quietly, try to negotiate, to gain time, the gendarmes are on the way here."

I grasped the schoolmaster's arm.

"Listen, I've got to get out, give me the key," I yelled at him, but he shook me off, and I shook the locked door in vain.

"The gendarmes? Who sent for the gendarmes?" I heard the baron say.

"I did," said the priest. "I've talked to Osnabrück three times today. At midday and then again this evening."

"You called the gendarmes, reverend father?" the baron called out. "So you knew at midday . . ."

"No, I knew nothing but guessed everything, I was afraid. I've always warned you, you think you're calling on God, but it's Moloch who will come. Moloch has come. Can't you hear him?"

Fists and cudgels started hammering on the door, and there were also blows with an axe. The baron picked up his revolver and turned to Federico.

"Go up to your room. Now," he ordered him.

"No," Federico replied.

This refusal made the baron wince as if he had been struck with a whip.

"You will go upstairs and lock yourself in your room," he repeated.

"No," said Federico.

"Federico," said Baron von Malchin, "have you forgotten what I taught you? The law of the old Empire says: The son who refuses his father obedience shall be eternally without honour, which he shall never regain."

"I'm staying here," said Federico.

That is how I saw the boy for the last time, and that is how I remember him, standing with arms folded in front of his chest, resting them on the huge Hohenstaufen sword, fearless and motionless, like a stone statue of his great ancestor.

"Open," a voice cried from outside the door, and I was thunderstruck, for the voice was Bibiche's. "Open, or we'll break down the door."

I think it was the baron himself who opened it. A dozen peasants, armed with axes and flails, knives and cudgels, burst into the hall, and one of the first was Bibiche – Bibiche with hate-filled eyes and a cold, hard expression on her lips, and behind her was Prince Praxatin, the last of the line of Rurik, waving a red flag and bellowing the words of the Internationale in Russian.

"Stop!" the baron shouted at the peasants. "Stop, or I fire. What do you mean by bursting in here like this?"

"We are the revolutionary council of the workers and peasants of Morwede. We have come to take what is ours," my landlord, the tailor, called out.

"You're rabble," the baron shouted at them. "You're rebels, drunken bandits."

"Awaken, damned of the earth," Prince Praxatin shouted, and the shopkeeper made his way to the door and called out to the peasants outside: "We've got him. He's here."

"Make war on the palaces," yelled Prince Praxatin. "Long live the economic liberation of the proletariat. Death to the landowners and their lackeys."

"String him up, string him up," peasants shouted outside. "There are plenty of trees here, and plenty of telegraph poles too."

"For heaven's sake be reasonable," the priest appealed to the mob.

"Death to the priest," someone yelled, and a woman appeared among the sea of faces, she had a knife in her hand and threatened the priest with it.

"Get back," the baron called out sharply, and there was a moment's silence. "Get back. One step forward, and I fire. If you have something to say to me, let one of you come forward and the others keep quiet. All right. And now one of you come forward. One of you only. Who is it to be?"

"Me," Bibiche called out. "Me."

Baron von Malchin leaned forward and looked her in the face.

"You, Kallisto?" he called out. "Are you going to speak in the name of this rabble?"

"I speak in the name of the peasants and workers of Morwede," Bibiche said. "I speak in the name of the toiling masses who suffer here as they do everywhere. I speak in the name of the exploited and oppressed."

Baron von Malchin stepped towards her.

"You cheated me, didn't you?" he said with icy calm. "Day after day you cheated me. So that was your work. What did you poison these people with? Confess."

He had seized her hand, but she tore herself away.

"Look at him," she called out to the peasants. "This is the parasite who sucks your blood. This is the man who has your last cow driven away when you can't pay the rent of your potato fields. There is no day on which you do not go hungry because of him, there is no single day when he does not enrich himself on your poverty. Now you're face to face with him and you can settle with him."

"That will do," said the baron. "First of all I have to settle with you. You have cheated and defrauded me, you have destroyed my life's work. Why did you do that? Who paid you?"

I am not sure I can describe with complete accuracy what happened next. Things may have happened in a different order. I saw a heavy object, perhaps an axe or a hammer, fly right past Baron von Malchin's head. He raised his revolver, aimed and fired, and the shot hit me. I had flung myself between him and Bibiche.

At first I did not realise I was wounded. The peasants surged forward, and I lost sight of the baron. I heard Federico shout: "Get back, get back." "People, people," the priest wailed, "this is murder. The gendarmes are coming." Prince Praxatin ran past me with blood streaming from his head.

The innkeeper, struck by a blow from the flat of Federico's sword, reeled and collapsed. The blacksmith picked up one of the heavy armchairs to hurl it at Federico, but I took the whisky bottle and smashed it on his hand. He yelled and dropped the chair.

Suddenly I felt a sharp pain in my shoulder. The room started heaving and going round and round. I saw a flail over my head, it rose into the air before coming down on me. "The gendarmes are here, the gendarmes are here," the priest shouted, and I heard signals being given by klaxon and orders being shouted, and then I lost consciousness.

TWENTY-THREE

I lay in bed, well wrapped up, the nurse had opened the window for a few minutes, and cold, wintery, fresh air had flooded into the room. It did me good. I had no more pain, I could even move my arm. The only thing that irritated me was that I could not shave. I could feel the stubble on my face, a state of affairs I have always found intolerable. I should have liked to get up and walk round the room, but the nurse would not let me, she said I must first ask the medical superintendent.

How I hated the woman. She sat by the window, noisily gulping her morning coffee, with her crocheting ready on the window sill. She looked at me over the coffeepot with something like disapproval on her simple face, evidently she wanted me to lie still or even go to sleep. But I couldn't sleep, I didn't feel tired, though I had lain awake nearly all night.

I had lain awake thinking. In my mind's eye I could see the manor house with wild vine growing up its reddish walls, the well and the garden pavilion, the square church tower and the village houses between which white mist always hung, morning and evening, day after day, and that wretched room of mine in which I had made love to Bibiche now struck me as a paradise lost. Bibiche. How she had changed on that dreadful night. What madness had come over her? And the villagers of Morwede – what had made them fall on Baron von Malchin like a pack of mad dogs?

I found no answer to these questions, and I gave up pondering and brooding. I felt as if a heavy stone lay on my breast from the weight of which there was no escape.

I did not go to sleep till morning.

The medical superintendent came in with his two assistants. This time they did not change my bandages.

"Well, how are we today?" the medical superintendent asked. "Did you sleep well? Any pain? And how's the appetite? Not too good, eh? Well, it'll come back eventually. Force yourself to eat a little. And there was something else I was going to ask you about – what was that story about a flail? You promised to tell me more about it."

"But you don't believe me," I said. "You don't want to believe me."

He stroked his pointed beard.

"That's a prejudice on your part," he said. "I believe my patients implicitly, on principle. My patients are always right."

He did not return to the subject. He gave the nurse some instructions about my diet and was about to walk out when I stopped him and asked him to send me a barber.

"I'll see to that," Dr Friebe said and made a note in his notebook.

He smiled.

"So vanity's setting in. You're beginning to worry about your appearance," he said. "That's a good sign, it means you're coming back to life again."

He went, and five minutes later Prince Praxatin appeared in my room in blue and white striped apron and with shaving stick and razor.

He looked annoyed, as if the job were extremely unwelcome, though he had often made himself busy in my room – he seemed to have to keep coming in to reassure himself that I had not recognised him. But he had always avoided coming close to me, and he glanced at me surreptitiously only when he thought he was unobserved. Or had I misconstrued his behaviour? Was he perhaps seeking an opportunity to talk to me unobserved? If he had anything to say to me, now was the time.

He bent over me, soaped me, and began shaving me – to my surprise he did so quite skilfully, he must have acquired the art here in the hospital, because at Morwede he had always had himself shaved before dinner by one of the two manservants.

When he had finished he held a small mirror in front of me. He had said nothing yet, but now I wanted to talk to him, I wanted to put an end to the farce and not let him go until he had answered my questions. I wanted to find out at last where Bibiche was and what had happened to the baron and Federico – he knew, and he was going to tell me.

"Who brought you here?" I asked quietly.

He acted as if I had not spoken.

"How did you get here?" I asked again.

He shrugged his shoulders, and then he said in that soft, singsong voice of his: "You wanted to be shaved. The doctor sent me to you."

At that I lost patience.

"You don't imagine I don't recognise you," I said sharply, but too quietly for the nurse to hear.

He looked embarrassed and avoided my eyes.

"You know me?" he said grumpily. "I'm afraid I don't know you. I've shaved you – do you need anything else? I have other gentlemen to shave."

"Arkady Fyodorovich," I said very quietly, "the last time I saw you you were singing the Internationale and carrying a red flag."

"What was I carrying?"

"A red flag."

This frightened him. He flushed and then turned quite pale.

"What I do in my spare time is nobody's business," he said quite loudly, and the nurse raised her head and listened. "I do my work here like everyone else."

He looked at me angrily. Then he got his things together, and turned once more before he reached the door.

"And in any case it's nobody's business what I do."

He walked out and slammed the door.

Later Dr Friebe came, sat on my bed, and began talking.

"Tell me," he suddenly said, "you had a row with our male nurse a little while ago. The man was quite upset, he came and complained to me about you. He said you objected to his politics. Good gracious me, everyone here knows that he carries the red flag in Communist demonstrations. He's a card-carrying member of the party. He's no shining light, of course, but he does his job here quite well and he's a thoroughly harmless individual."

"I don't regard him as harmless," I said. "He's a sham, here he plays the part of being not very strong in the head, I don't know what his object is."

"Oh? Really?" Dr Friebe exclaimed. "Where do you know him from?"

"The place where I was the village doctor."

"Oh? Where was that?"

"Morwede."

"Morwede," he repeated thoughtfully. "Yes there really is a place called that. We once had a patient from there, he worked in the sugar factory."

"There's no sugar factory at Morwede," I said.

"Oh, yes there is, there must be. So you met our male nurse at Morwede. That's interesting. What was he doing there?"

"He was the manager of an estate."

"Oh, stop it," Dr Friebe said. "He knows as much about agriculture as I know about hunting kangaroos. Perhaps at a pinch he might be able to tell an ox from a cow. He the manager of an estate?"

"You don't believe me," I said resignedly. "There's no point in going on talking about it. Perhaps you won't believe this either – do you remember a Greek girl student named Kallisto Tsanaris who worked with us at the Bacteriological Institute?"

"Yes," he said, "I remember her very well."

"I met her again at Morwede."

"Oh," he said. "She's married and living in Osnabrück. Are

138

you quite sure of what you're saying? Did you talk to her at Morwede?"

I couldn't help laughing.

"Did I talk to her?" I exclaimed. "I slept with her there."

I immediately regretted having said this, I could have kicked myself. I had given away my secret and put Bibiche and me in his hands.

"You won't repeat that," I said to him. "I'll break your neck if you ever mention it to anyone."

He smiled, and made a gesture intended to placate me.

"Come, come," he said, "I'm discreet, that's something that can be taken for granted between us men. So you slept with her?"

"Yes, for one night only. Or don't you believe that either?"

"Oh, yes I do," he said very seriously. "Why should I disbelieve you? You wanted her, you had to have her, and so you did have her. You achieved the impossible – in dream, Amberg, in a feverish dream while you lay there in delirium."

An icy paroxysm crept slowly up my body, a cold hand seemed to be feeling for my heart in order to stop it. I wanted to shout, but I could make no sound. I stared at this man sitting on the edge of my bed, he looked as if he were speaking the truth, but something inside me rose in protest. No, no, no, he's lying, don't listen to him, he wants to steal Bibiche from you, he wants to steal everything from you, away with him, get him out of my sight, I don't want to see him any more – and then suddenly I grew quite weak and tired, I was so tired I could hardly breathe, a deep discouragement came over me, I knew he was telling the truth, Bibiche had never been mine.

"Don't look so upset, Amberg," said Dr Friebe. "Don't take it so much to heart. Dreams are lavish with what tight-fisted reality withholds from us. And this so-called reality – what remains of it? Even what we have really had grows pale and shadowy and ultimately fades away just as dreams do."

"Go away," I said, and shut my eyes. I wanted to be alone, every word that he said hurt me.

He rose to his feet.

"You'll come to terms with it," he said as he went away. "Sooner or later you would have found out for yourself. Tomorrow you'll feel quite differently about it."

When I was alone I began for the first time to realise what had happened to me, and only then did despair get the better of me.

Why go on living, why did I wake up? I groaned and wailed to myself. They had used their skill to bring me back to the desolation of everyday life, it was over, I had lost everything, I was destitute. Did I have to go on living? Bibiche, Morwede, Our Lady's Fire — all of it had been nothing but the stuff of dreams and delirium. Memories were already getting confused, pictures in my mind were growing dim and indistinct, words were fading away, the dream eluded me. Oblivion came down like mist on the houses and people of Morwede.

It grew dark inside me. Let my eyes close and let me not wake up. It is not necessary to go on living. Bibiche . . .

"Praised be Jesus Christ," the nurse suddenly said loudly.

"For ever and ever, amen," said a voice, and I winced, because I recognised it.

I opened my eyes. The village priest of Morwede was standing by my bed.

TWENTY-FOUR

"Is it you?" I exclaimed in amazement, and felt his cassock.
"How can that be? Is it really you, or . . . ?"

He solemnly and lengthily cleared his throat into his blue
check handkerchief, and then he nodded to me.

"You seem surprised at my coming to see you," he said.
"Didn't you expect me to? I heard you had recovered conscious-
ness – it was a human duty to come and see you, after all. Did
I give you a fright, perhaps, or awaken unpleasant memories?"

I sat up and looked at him. I noticed the slight smell of
snuff and incense that came from his cassock – it was real.
Where's Dr Friebe? I exclaimed inside myself. Why isn't he
here?

"Yes, you've had a very bad time," the parish priest of
Morwede went on, "but now, thanks be to the Almighty, it's
as good as over. You'll be able to leave the hospital in a few
days. But believe me, it was a dreadful moment for me too
when I saw you collapse."

"Where did I collapse?"

"In the hall. Just when the gendarmes arrived. Don't you
remember?"

"You're the parish priest of Morwede, aren't you?" I said.
"You came down the stairs and said the house was surrounded,
and then the peasants arrived with flails and axes. Your cassock
was torn. That really happened, didn't it, or did I only dream
it?"

"Dream it?" the priest said, and shook his head. "What gave
you that idea? Unfortunately it was all as real and true as I'm

standing here. Did someone perhaps try and tell you that you only dreamt it?"

I nodded.

"Yes. The doctors try to make me believe that five weeks ago I was knocked down by a car in the station square here in Osnabrück, and that I lay unconscious here in this room for five weeks and have never been to Morwede. And if you hadn't come here, reverend father . . ."

"That doesn't surprise me, I was expecting something of the sort," the priest interrupted me. "Let me tell you that there are forces at work interested in hushing up the matter, and the prospects of that happening are by no means unfavourable, for this is one of those cases in which public and private interests coincide. In higher quarters there is no desire to admit publicly to an outbreak of revolutionary feeling among the peasantry. So you will appreciate that the trouble was purely local and devoid of political significance. It was quickly put down, the peasants have gone back to their fields and ploughs, and so grass could be allowed to grow over the matter – but for the awkward fact that there is an extremely inconvenient witness in the hospital here. He might end by coming forward and talking, and then inquiries would have to be pursued further, and perhaps some individuals might have to be prosecuted. Now do you understand why they want to persuade you that everything you went through was merely a feverish dream? There are witnesses who speak and witnesses who must remain silent. And you, doctor, will remain silent, won't you?"

"Now I understand everything," I said, and felt quite light-hearted and cheerful again. "They want to rob me of a part of my life. But you and I, reverend father, know I haven't been dreaming, but that I really was at Morwede."

"Yes, we both know," the priest said.

"And Baron von Malchin, won't he talk?"

The priest's lips moved as in silent prayer.

"No, Baron von Malchin will not talk. Baron von Malchin is dead, he died of heart failure in the midst of the tumult.

Don't begrudge him that easy end. A minute later his peasants would have beaten him to death."

I fell silent. I did not dare ask the next question.

"Yes, doctor, the dream of resurrecting the Hohenstaufen empire is over. There's no Kyffhäuser, there's no secret emperor any longer. Federico? I sent him back to his father in Bergamo. He's going to be a carpenter. The little girl Elsie is at a boarding school in Switzerland, she doesn't yet know her father is dead. One day perhaps she may remember the companion of her youth and fetch him from his workshop. Or perhaps she won't."

"And she?" I asked. The question had been on my lips the whole time. "What has happened to her?"

The priest smiled. He guessed it was Bibiche I was asking about.

"She's safe," he said. "Perhaps you didn't know she was married, she didn't like talking about it, she wasn't living with her husband. Now she has gone back to him, here in Osnabrück. All the efforts to hush things up originate with him. He's an important personality in the town here, an influential man. Don't try to thwart him. You'd be alone in the struggle, one man against so many. Me? Good heavens, no, doctor, you can't count on me. When I leave this building you will notice that no one will have seen me. When I've gone, I'll have been nothing but a part of your dream. Be wise, doctor, if the doctors again tell you that you were in a twilight state when you had that dream about Morwede, accept it and leave it at that. Remember that all this is happening for that woman's sake, don't forget that. Weren't you in love with her once, or am I mistaken?"

"But why did she turn on the baron?" I asked. "Why did she destroy his life's work?"

"She didn't," the priest said, shaking his head. "She was completely innocent of the assault on him. She was merely carrying out his ideas."

"Then there was an error in his calculations. How could he

go astray like that? That dreadful outcome of his experiment."

"The experiment was successful, doctor, he made no mistake. He wanted to lead the world back to faith . . . The Church of Christ is immutable and eternal. But faith? Every age has its faith, and the faith of our time, I've known for a long time, the faith of our age is . . ."

He made a helpless gesture, and there was sorrow, weariness and deep resignation in his face.

"Revolution?" I suggested quietly and hesitantly. "Is that the faith of our time?"

The priest did not answer.

I closed my eyes and thought. Revolution. The dream of a violent reorganisation of things. Did not that faith, like any other, have its evangelists and its Bible, its myths and its dogmas, its priests and its sects, its martyrs and its paradise? Was not its teaching, like any new teaching, persecuted and suppressed by the world's rulers? Did it not live secretly in the hearts of many who were forced to deny it with their lips? Streams of blood had been shed for its sake all over the world. Was it the Bible of our time or its Moloch?

"Reverend father," I said, "help me. What is the faith of our time?"

There was no reply.

I opened my eyes and sat up.

The village priest of Morwede had gone, leaving behind only an odour of snuff and incense.

"Nurse," I said, "please call the gentleman back."

The nurse looked up from her crocheting.

"What gentleman?"

"The clerical gentleman who has just walked out."

"Nobody has been here."

"I was talking to a priest only a minute ago. He was standing by my bed. He has just walked out. A spiritual gentleman, a priest."

The nurse took the thermometer, shook it, and put it under my armpit.

144

"A priest?" she said. "No, nobody's been here. You've been talking to yourself."

I looked at her, first surprised and then angry – and then at last I understood. Of course. He foresaw it. When I leave this building, notice that no one will want to have seen me, he had said. That is exactly what had happened. How right he had been.

What was his advice? I should say yes and accept it. Very well, then.

"You're quite right, nurse," I said. "I was talking to myself. I often do that, it's a bad habit, I know. Is the medical superintendent coming here again today? Please tell him I want to talk to him urgently."

The medical superintendent was standing in the doorway.

"Well?" he said. "You sent for me. Is anything the matter? Are you feverish?"

"No, there's no fever," I said. "I just wanted to tell you that I now distinctly remember how the accident happened. I was crossing the station square, there was a frightful din, I stopped and picked up a pamphlet I had dropped, there was a honk behind me, and it was then that the car must have run me down."

"And that story about the flail?"

"I must have dreamt it."

"Thank God," he said, and his relief was obvious. "Listen," he said, "I was seriously worried about you. I was afraid of another brain haemorrhage and more mental aberration. But that danger seems to have passed. All that's necessary now is for you to get your strength back. I think that in about a week's time I'll be able to discharge you to be looked after at home. Would that suit you?"

TWENTY-FIVE

A week later I walked up two flights of stairs with the aid of a stick and went to the medical superintendent's office to say goodbye.

He got up from his desk and came to meet me.

"Well, there you are," he said. "You've made an astonishingly quick recovery these last few days, you're hardly recognisable. So you're leaving us today? When I think of the state you were in when you were brought here. No, my dear colleague, there's nothing to thank us for, we owe it to your sturdy constitution that it has ended so satisfactorily – what I did was no more than my duty. Yes, it happens to be my speciality, that I admit. So you're taking the midday train? If you should ever pass through Osnabrück again . . ."

"Eduard, won't you introduce me to the gentleman?" said a voice behind me, I turned, and it was Bibiche.

We looked at each other. Nothing in her face betrayed any emotion. Could she control herself to that extent? Or had she known I was going to be there?

"Dr Amberg, my wife," said the medical superintendent. "Have you left the car below? It's rather early, I still have some work to do. Dr Amberg has been a patient here until today. The result of an accident in the station square. Well, what happened? You tell us, doctor."

"I was run down by a car," I explained.

The medical superintendent stroked his moustache in satisfaction.

"So you were not struck by a flail, were you? That was

146

his fixed idea, let me tell you. He was convinced of it for days."

He laughed. Bibiche looked at me with big, serious eyes.

"Fracture of the base of the skull and brain haemorrhage," the medical superintendent went on.

"Was it as bad as that?" Bibiche said to me, and I could have hugged her for the sympathy and sorrow in her voice.

"Yes, it really wasn't very simple at all," the medical superintendent answered for me. "He kept us busy for six whole weeks."

"You won't have very happy memories of that time, will you?" Bibiche said, and her eyes told me how anxiously she awaited my answer.

"I shall never forget that time," I replied. "I shall take away with me a great and beautiful memory."

And I bent forward, and said very quietly: "And you, Bibiche?"

Quietly though I had spoken, the medical superintendent heard.

"You know my wife?" he said, turning to me. "You know her nickname?"

"I've been racking my brains the whole time about where I met this gentleman before," Bibiche said quickly.

She looked at me, and her eyes pleaded: Be careful, don't give me away, he suspects what there was between us, and if he knew . . .

No, Bibiche, have no fear, I shan't give you away.

I said: "I had the pleasure of working with this lady at the Bacteriological Institute."

Bibiche smiled.

"Of course," she said, "how stupid of me not to remember straight away. It wasn't so very long ago, either."

"No," I said, "it wasn't so very long ago."

We fell silent, and for a moment we both thought of Morwede and the wretched little room approached by a creaking staircase.

147

The medical superintendent cleared his throat. Bibiche offered me her hand.

"Bon voyage, doctor, and . . ."

She hesitated and sought for one last thing to say to me.

"And think well of us when you call us to mind," she said.

I bent over her hand.

"Thank you," I said, and felt her hand trembling in mine. Bibiche knew what I was thanking her for.

I walked across the courtyard. Bibiche was at the window, and she was looking at me, I knew. I knew without looking back, I felt her eyes on me.

I walked slowly. The snow was beginning to melt, and the sun had appeared between the clouds. Water dripped from the roofs. The air was mild, and it looked as if today might be the beginning of spring.